Leah's Amish Love

Stephanie Swift

Published by Trellis Publishing, 2021.

This is a work of fiction. Similarities to real people, places, or events are entirely coincidental.

LEAH'S AMISH LOVE

First edition. July 15, 2021.

Copyright © 2021 Stephanie Swift.

ISBN: 979-8224511976

Written by Stephanie Swift.

LEAH'S AMISH LOVE
STEPHANIE SWIFT

Leah King wrapped her arms around the large wicker basket and tried with all her might to hoist it off the floorboard of her wagon, but it was no use. The basket refused to budge. She stepped back and wiped her brow with her dress sleeve before putting her hands on her hips to assess the situation.

"How do they make it look so easy?" she muttered.

The basket was loaded to the brim with individually wrapped pieces of cheese, freshly made on her family's farm, but it was the first time she'd delivered them to Walnut Creek by herself. Normally, her father or his employee, Luke, would accompany her, but summer was an especially busy time of the year on the farm, and today she was on her own while they worked overtime.

Everything was going smoothly until it came time to unload the basket. There was no way she could pick it up and prop it on her shoulder the way her father and Luke did, but she was starting to wonder if she would be able to lift it at all.

Leah scanned the sidewalk to make sure none of the town patrons were gawking at her before she climbed onto the wagon's mounting step. She hoped that using a different angle would work to her advantage, but as she leaned over and pulled and tugged on the basket handle, it still wouldn't move.

"Do you need some help?"

Startled, Leah grabbed the side of the wagon to keep from falling. When she glanced behind her to see who offered their assistance, she was surprised to find a young English man standing in the doorway of the grocery store she was attempting to deliver her goods to. She hated to admit defeat, but she couldn't keep trying to win a losing battle when it was nearing dusk and she needed to be on her way home.

"*Yah,*" she replied, shyly. "*Denki.*"

The stranger was so tall it took only a couple of steps before he reached her side, and when he put his hands around her waist to help her down, the gesture caught her completely off guard. Besides an occasional hug from her father and grandfather, no man had ever touched her before, and the way his strong hands gripped her body made her cheeks hot.

After setting her on the ground, he lifted the basket from the wagon in one fluent movement, as if the heavy load of cheese weighed nothing. He turned to her and tilted his head toward the store, and Leah led the way, trying desperately not to stare at him too long so he wouldn't catch her blushing.

"I'm guessing you're Leah," he remarked. "I was told you would be coming by today with a delivery."

She was very much aware of his towering presence behind her as they made their way to the checkout counter. From what she could tell, the store was empty of customers, and the owners, the Nelson's, were nowhere to be seen.

"*Yah*. I'm Leah King. I don't recall seeing you here before. Have you worked with the Nelson's long?"

He set the basket on the counter and smiled at her. Even though she tried not to ogle him, she couldn't help but notice how handsome he was. His hair was brown with a few sun-kissed streaks of blonde throughout, and his eyes were the lightest shade of blue she'd ever seen before. He looked to be about her age, but she couldn't be certain.

"I guess you could say I've known them awhile. They're my parents."

Leah's jaw slacked. She'd been selling her cheese and other homemade goods to the Nelson's almost a year now, and she had no idea they had a child.

"I'm Bryan, by the way."

He held out a hand and Leah tentatively shook it. His skin was hot to the touch, and she couldn't help but notice he held her hand longer than necessary.

"It's nice meeting you," she replied.

He had a charming smile that bordered on mischievous, and Leah slipped her hand from his grasp to break the connection. She'd seen too many friends from her small Amish community fall in love with English men, which caused a great deal of controversy with the elders of the church, and she wasn't about to let the same thing happen to her. Leah looked away and started unpacking the basket so she could be on her way – quickly.

"It's nice meeting you too. I try to help out as much as I can while I'm home from college during the summer break, so we'll probably see a lot of each other over the next couple of months."

Her heart raced at the possibility – a girly response that annoyed her a great deal. Leah worked faster to finish unloading the basket, and all the while, Bryan never turned his attention elsewhere.

"You got here just in time. I've had several customers ask me today when this was going to be restocked. It sells fast."

His comment made Leah smile. She took immense pride in everything she created, and it did her heart good knowing others were enjoying it so much.

"Do you make anything else besides cheese?" he asked.

Bryan reached his hands inside the basket and helped her stack the last remaining cheese on the countertop. When his fingers brushed against her own, she felt an electric jolt course through her entire body, which nearly knocked her off her feet. She swallowed hard before trusting herself to speak.

"There's an elderly woman who lives a few miles from here who uses our sheep wool to make blankets and hats, and there are a couple of other grocer's here in Walnut Creek who buy our cow's milk."

He asked several more questions about the family business, and he seemed genuinely interested, but Leah tried not to dwell on it too much. He could've been just making small-talk, like he probably did with every other person who visited the store.

Bryan propped his elbows on the counter and leaned in close, prompting Leah to take a cautious step backward. When the doorbell jingled and a customer walked in, she expelled a sigh of relief.

"I should be going. I have a long ride home, and it will be dark soon. Please tell Mr. and Mrs. Nelson I said 'hello' and that I'll have more cheese ready by the end of next week."

She turned to leave, but Bryan grabbed her arm and stopped her.

"Wait," he said. "Don't forget this."

He handed her an envelope with her payment inside, and Leah's face flushed with embarrassment as she silently reprimanded herself for being so enamored with her new friend that she forgot it was strictly a business visit. She thanked him and took the envelope from his hands, trying very hard to avoid any skin-to-skin contact.

"Maybe the next time you're in town we can go to the coffee shop next door for a quick cup of coffee," he suggested.

Leah gave him a curious look. There were so many beautiful English women in Walnut Creek. Why was he so interested in an Amish woman?

"Alright," she replied.

As soon as the word passed her lips, she wished she could take it back. *Was she insane?* If her parents found out she said yes to such a thing with someone outside their community, they would be extremely disappointed in her.

When Bryan left to tend to his customer, Leah quickly departed Nelson's Grocery before she said something else she regretted.

* * * *

"Have you ever heard the saying 'A watched pot never boils'?"

Luke Sommer stopped pacing by the barn window and looked at his boss, Mr. Matthew King, who was busy sweeping one of the stalls a few feet away. Mr. King wasn't looking at him, but Luke couldn't miss the huge smirk on his face.

"I know...I know..." he replied. "I'm being ridiculous."

Mr. King rested his broom against the stall door and looked over the side of the wooden slats in his direction.

"You're worried, and I understand that, but Leah is nineteen years old and a grown woman. Her mother and I aren't panicked, so you shouldn't be either. She'll be here soon."

Since his father's passing nine years prior, Mr. King had become more of a father figure to Luke than any of his uncles or grandfathers, and if anyone knew how deeply his feelings ran for Leah, her father certainly did. However, finding the courage to tell Leah was something else entirely. Even though they'd known each other since childhood, he still tripped over his own tongue whenever she was near.

He hated not being able to ride with her to Walnut Creek, but it couldn't be helped. They were knee-deep in customer orders, and it took every minute of the day for him and Mr. King to catch up. Luke glanced out the window as the sun sank on the horizon. It would be dark soon and Leah should've been back by now. The thought that something terrible may have happened to her made his insides churn. He would not let her go to Walnut Creek by herself ever again, even if that meant working overtime for the next few weeks or even months.

The sound of horse hooves on the main road in front of the King homestead made his heart skip a beat. Finally! As he took off running in the direction of the door, he caught a glimpse of Mr. King picking up his broom to start sweeping again.

"I hate to say I told you so, but..." the elder man laughed.

Luke ignored him and rushed toward the door, slowing his pace only when he stepped outside. Even though he was happy to see her, he didn't want to appear *too* excited. Leah turned off the main road and into the King driveway and waved to Luke when she saw him approaching. She brought the horse and wagon to a stop beside the house, and as Luke reached her side, he held out his hand to help her down.

The bonnet she wore was lopsided and several tendrils of her hair had escaped from the loose ponytail gathered at the nape of her neck. The strands caressed her forehead and cheeks, and it took a great deal of willpower to keep his hands to himself and not brush them away from her face.

She was so beautiful, and her smile melted his heart into a giant puddle of mush. The effect she had on him was unlike anything he'd ever felt before. Perhaps soon he'd be able to tell her just that.

"Going by the big smile on your face, and the way your bonnet is barely hanging on to your head, I'm guessing you flew home."

She giggled at his remark, and the sweet sound reached inside his chest and gripped him hard.

"I was trying to get home before dark," she whispered. "Don't tell father."

Luke took the reins and led the horse and wagon toward the barn as Leah fell in step beside him. She removed her bonnet and smoothed her hair in place before putting it back on and tying it securely.

"Did you have any problems?" he asked.

She straightened the apron around her waist and shrugged her shoulders. "Not unless you count the basket I couldn't lift because it felt like a ton of bricks."

Luke stopped in his tracks. He was so used to going with her to deliver orders that he never even considered the basket might be too heavy when he loaded it inside the wagon that morning. "I'm sorry. I didn't even think about that. How did you get it out of the wagon?"

She kept walking, and Luke took a couple of long strides to catch up with her.

"It's alright," she replied. "The Nelson's son, Bryan, helped me."

It was probably just his imagination getting the best of him again, but the sing-song way she said his name put Luke's senses on high alert. She smiled when she said it too, and she twirled the strings on her bonnet around and around her fingers while looking up at the sky. She seemed oblivious to his presence, and he cleared his throat to try and snap her out of her daydream.

"I didn't know the Nelson's had a son. How old is he?" he asked, as nonchalantly as he could.

Leah furrowed a brow. "I'm not sure, but he's in college, so I'm guessing he's about our age."

Luke frowned. That didn't sound good. He wanted to find out more about this Bryan person, but he didn't want to push the subject too hard either. They'd confided in each other many times through the years, and he was afraid to jeopardize that closeness by asking too many questions. Still, it was hard to deny how her behavior changed when she mentioned his name, and that alone made his heart ache.

"Luke, can I ask you something personal?"

His whole body tensed. Any other time he would have jumped at the chance to have such a conversation with Leah, but something in her tone of voice made him leery of what she might ask.

"*Yah*," he replied, hesitantly.

She didn't say anything right away, and so they walked in silence for several agonizing seconds. They were within a few feet of the barn when she clutched his arm to make him stop. When she spoke, it was in a low whisper, like she was afraid her father might overhear, and he had to lean in close to catch every word.

"Have you ever been attracted to someone...to someone *not* like us?" she asked.

Luke immediately stood up straight and tried to take a deep breath. It felt like someone had punched him in the gut, and it was hard to breathe normally. His emotions teetered dangerously back and forth between anger and sadness, and he didn't trust himself to answer her without saying something that might hurt her feelings. She didn't mention his name, but it was blatantly obvious she was referring to Bryan.

"*Neh*, I haven't. I don't find English women attractive because during my *rumspringa* I saw firsthand how greedy they can be."

She crossed her arms over her chest and thrust her chin out.

"I'm sure they're not *all* like that, Luke. You're being judgmental."

It wouldn't do for him to try and explain because he knew very well once she made her mind up about someone or something, there was no changing it. He looked at the ground and shuffled his feet. In just a matter of minutes his entire world had been turned upside down. Maybe it was his own fault for foolishly thinking that he and Leah might find their way to each other someday.

"I've only been in love with one woman and she's one of us. I believe that's the way God intended it to be. We're so different from them, Leah. Maybe I am being judgmental, but I just don't see how it could work. Don't you want a lasting relationship, like your parents?"

She sighed before nodding. "Of course, I do."

He touched her arm, and when she looked up at him, he could tell that his response wasn't what she hoped for. He wasn't going to lie to her though, even if it meant risking their friendship.

"Then please don't go down this path, Leah. It's not worth it."

She started walking toward the barn again. "I didn't say I *was* attracted to someone, Luke. I was just curious."

He knew better, but he didn't argue with her. Honestly, there were times he felt like he knew her better than she knew herself.

Leah opened a large sliding metal door on the barn and he ushered the horse inside so he could unhitch the wagon and be on his way home. His heart ached, and he just wanted to be alone. When Luke walked by Leah, she grabbed his arm and stopped him again.

"Wait! Who is this woman you were talking about – the one you were in love with? Why haven't you told me about her?"

Her curiosity twisted the dagger in his heart, and Luke pulled himself free of her grasp. He wanted to tell her the truth, but it felt like the wrong time, especially after everything they'd just discussed.

Luckily, Mr. King walked over to join them at that time, giving him the reprieve he needed.

While Leah filled him in on her day, Luke walked to the opposite end of the barn where he unhitched the wagon and led the horse to its stall. After one last glimpse in their direction, he exited through one of the side doors and quietly slipped away.

* * * *

"I don't need a babysitter."

Leah rolled her eyes heavenward as Luke walked around the wagon for the hundredth time, making sure the reins were secure and the baskets of cheese and milk were safely nestled in the back.

"Why do you think I'm babysitting you?" he asked. "This isn't any different from the numerous other times we rode to Walnut Creek together."

He kept his eyes focused on what he was doing, which was probably for the best. If her face portrayed her emotions, Luke might be highly offended. She'd worked hard all week to have the cheese ready before schedule so she could see Bryan sooner, and her plans were ruined in one fell swoop when Luke volunteered to go with her and her father didn't object.

"I managed fine on my own last week. You should stay here in case father needs you."

Luke climbed up in the wagon and took the reins as he sat down beside her.

"Is there a reason you don't want me to go, Leah?"

She wished she could tell him, but after discovering his feelings toward English people, she was afraid he might rat her out to her parents, and that would open a whole new can of worms she wasn't ready to deal with.

"*Neh*, of course there isn't." Leah laced her fingers together and sighed. "Never mind. You wouldn't understand, so let's just go."

Thankfully, he didn't push the matter, but they spent the rest of the long drive barely speaking to each other. When they did talk, it was just idle chit chat to pass the time. There was a strained awkwardness between them that was very disconcerting, and Leah knew deep down it was her fault. Since meeting Bryan, nothing felt the same, even her friendship with Luke. If he felt the same distance between them, he didn't mention it.

When Walnut Creek came into view, Leah sat up straighter and made one last sweep over her clothing. She ran her palms along her hair to smooth it down, and she pulled the strings on her bonnet to make sure it wasn't crooked on top of her head again. She couldn't remember a time when she'd ever felt so jittery, and she breathed in deeply to try and calm her nerves.

"I'll drop the milk off at the Anderson's store first," Luke stated.

Leah frowned. If Luke and the Anderson couple carried on a lengthy conversation, like they often did, she would be a nervous wreck by the time they made it to the Nelson's. She'd waited all week to see Bryan again, and she didn't want to put it off any longer.

"Why don't we go to the Nelson's instead? It's closer anyway."

She saw him clench his jaw, and he gripped the reins so tightly his knuckles turned white, but in the end, he steered the horse toward the Nelson's store. When he came to a stop in front of it, she was the first one out of the wagon. They walked to the back and removed the sheet covering the milk and cheese just as she heard the jingle of the door opening.

Leah was almost afraid to look up. What if it was Mr. or Mrs. Nelson and Bryan wasn't there? The idea bothered her a lot more than she cared to admit, but those thoughts were quickly vanquished when someone appeared by her side and she heard a familiar voice.

"Hello Leah."

Bryan.

When she turned to look at him, her body flooded with warmth. He looked so handsome, and she detected a faint scent of cologne, which drifted past her nose and made her knees wobble. Her tongue felt like it was glued to the top of her mouth, but Luke had no trouble at all as he stepped in between them and introduced himself.

"Luke Sommer," he announced. He held out his hand and Bryan cast a confusing glance between him and Leah before shaking it. She felt like swatting Luke on the arm and pushing him out of the way. If he was trying to make a good first impression, he was going about it the wrong way. Then again, he said he didn't care for English people, so perhaps acting like a jerk was his goal.

"Bryan Nelson. It's nice meeting you. Are you Leah's brother?"

She stifled a laugh, but Luke was anything but amused, and Leah knew she should intervene before he did something foolish. "We're not related. Luke works for my father."

She made a move to pick up one of the baskets loaded with cheese, but Bryan stepped up and gently moved her hands away. "Here. Let me help you with that."

He lifted the basket and started for the door, and Leah spun around on her heel and glared at Luke. "Please be nice."

He ignored her plea as he picked up the remaining basket of cheese, but she didn't miss the resentful look he gave her before following Bryan. She couldn't understand why he was being so unreasonable, but it was wearing on her nerves.

When Leah walked inside the store, she caught a glimpse of Bryan and Mrs. Nelson at the checkout counter. At first, she'd hoped Bryan would be manning the store alone again, but with Luke's unpredictable behavior, she was kind of relieved Bryan's mother was there to alleviate any awkwardness.

"Leah! It's so good to see you," she called. "And you too, Luke."

Her smile was lovely and lit up the room. Luke placed his basket on the counter before taking off his hat and saying "hello". The four of them proceeded to unload the baskets, and Mrs. Nelson talked the entire time while Bryan kept sneaking glances in Leah's direction. She tried to avoid his gaze to keep from blushing, but she failed miserably. When the baskets were emptied, he motioned for her to follow him, and she was grateful Mrs. Nelson talked incessantly to Luke and kept him preoccupied.

Leah walked with Bryan to the opposite side of the store, and he took her hand and pulled her behind a tall row of shelves where they couldn't be seen or heard. When they were alone at last, he didn't let go right away, and Leah felt the butterflies do somersaults inside her stomach as he caressed her hand with his thumb.

"Hi," he whispered with a smile.

"Hello," she replied, trying her best not to giggle like a giddy schoolgirl.

Bryan propped his arm against one of the shelves and leaned in to her. "I've been looking forward to seeing you again."

They were so close she could feel his breath on her face, and there was a moment where she thought he might kiss her, and the possibility terrified her. She'd never been intimate with a man before – not even something as innocent as holding hands. In her community, such things were strictly forbidden unless a couple intended to marry, so she had very little experience when it came to the opposite sex.

"I was hoping we could get that cup of coffee today," he said.

Leah could faintly hear Mrs. Nelson talking to Luke, and she looked toward the front door, wondering if it might be possible to sneak next door to the coffee shop without being spotted. The bell would give them away though, and unfortunately, there was no way around it.

"I'm not sure that will be possible unless I can sneak away from my house."

She said it jokingly, but Bryan's expression became deathly serious. "Could you do that?"

It surprised her that he would suggest it, but it shocked her even more when she started considering it. Dozens of different scenarios raced through her mind at once, but none of them seemed doable. If she went through with it and her parents found out, they would never forgive her. They could even go so far as shunning her if they discovered she was sneaking around with an English man.

"I'll see what I can do, but I can't promise anything."

Bryan closed the small gap between them, and when he reached out to touch her face, Leah held her breath.

"Ready to go?"

The sound of Luke's booming voice made her jump, almost completely out of her skin, and she immediately dropped Bryan's hand and moved away from him.

"The Anderson's are probably waiting on us."

Leah felt the heat course through her veins as her temper flared. "Can you please do it by yourself? Bryan and I were discussing something."

Luke stuffed his hands inside his trouser pockets. "I'll wait."

Bryan's expression was a mixture of amusement and annoyance, and Leah grabbed his hand and pulled him down the aisle and away from Luke so they wouldn't be overheard.

"I'm so sorry," she said.

Bryan brought her hand to his lips and kissed the back of it, and the sweet gesture made her swoon.

"It's okay," he softly murmured. "I'm here every day, so please try and come back soon. I want to see you again, Leah...preferably, alone."

She nodded, but she didn't agree to anything or make a promise she couldn't keep. Luke didn't leave his stance at the other end of the aisle, and he kept pacing back and forth like a caged lion, so she said "goodbye" to Bryan and turned to leave before Luke decided to try and intervene again.

As soon as she stepped outside, he was on her heels. She refused to say another word to him though, but she was determined to get to the bottom of his hostility once and for all before the night was over.

* * * *

Luke was angry, disappointed...and hurt.

Later that afternoon, on the drive home, he did everything possible to try and keep the image of Bryan standing close to Leah and kissing her hand out of his mind, but it was no use, and the more he dwelled on it, the angrier it made him. She hadn't said two words to him since leaving Walnut Creek, and she sat so close to the edge of the seat, he was afraid a sudden move might send her flying off the wagon.

"Why are you going so fast?" she asked.

Because of horse's hooves pounding loudly on the gravel road, he didn't hear it the first time she asked, but he did when she repeated herself.

"I'm ready to get home," he answered, his voice stoic and flat.

Leah slid across the seat and took the reins from him, and when she pulled up on them and brought the horse to a sudden halt, he had to grip to the side of the wagon to keep from being hurled forward. When the horse came to a complete stop, she threw the reins down and turned to face him, and he was surprised to see tears in her eyes.

"Luke! What is wrong with you?"

He looked up at the sky before taking a long, deep breath. He knew this conversation was bound to happen sometime, but he hoped it would be under different circumstances. He envisioned telling her he loved her and then her confessing she felt the same way, but he knew there was no chance of that happening. Not only was it obvious she considered him just a good friend, but Bryan was in the picture now.

"There's nothing wrong, Leah."

She moved to her end of the seat again and crossed her arms over her chest. "I don't believe that for a second. Please tell me what I've done to make you so angry."

A tear escaped and rolled down her cheek, and Luke felt like a heel for making her upset. The temperature had dropped as the sun began making its descent in the west, and he caught her shivering. He reached behind them and picked up one of the blankets from the back of the wagon, and as he wrapped it around her shoulders, she didn't attempt to stop him.

"We should go. I don't want you getting sick."

He went for the reins, but she wrapped a hand around his arm and prevented him from picking them up. Despite the chill in the air, warmth radiated from her hand and seeped into his bones.

"Not until you tell me what's bothering you," she said.

They were the only people on the road, which wasn't unusual since it was nearing nighttime. It was the perfect opportunity to tell her how he felt, but Leah was the only woman he'd ever loved, so he had no experience when it came to romance and matters of the heart.

Luke closed his eyes. There was only one place he could think of to start.

"I love you, Leah."

He heard her suck in a breath, but he kept going, knowing if he stopped, he might never find the courage again. "I've loved you since the first time I saw you playing on the tire swing at school when we were just six years old. I don't remember my life before I fell in love with you. It's become a part of me...as natural and important as breathing."

He opened his eyes, but he didn't look at her. If he saw anything that resembled pain, anger, or confusion in her gaze, it would devastate him, and he couldn't risk that. He'd come too far to turn back now.

"I've prayed so hard for so long for God to bring us together, and when I see something threatening that dream, I get angry. When I heard you talk about Bryan, and I saw the way you two looked at each other...I fell apart," he confessed. "I'm so sorry, Leah. I shouldn't have acted that way toward you. All I've ever wanted is to see you happy, even if it's not with me, and if Bryan makes you happy then I would never stand in the way of that."

He knew he was taking a huge risk, but he touched Leah's cheek and slid his fingertips along her jaw, before he changed his mind. Knowing it might be the last time she allowed him anywhere near her, he was willing to take the risk.

"I just don't want to see you hurt. You and I both know what will happen if you pursue this, and I can't bear to think of my life without you in it. Please just promise me you'll pray over this before you do something you might regret."

Leah stopped crying, but the sadness never left her beautiful face. "Why have you never told me this before?"

He kept caressing her cheek, and he smiled at her, hoping it would in turn help brighten her mood. "I didn't want to risk losing your friendship. I don't want to lose that...ever...even if you never feel the same way about me as I feel about you."

The tears began to well in her eyes again. "Luke..."

He hushed her tears by kissing her gently on the forehead, and neither of them spoke again during the remainder of the drive to her house. He was spent...empty...and he needed to be alone. As much as it upset him, he knew the right thing to do was distance himself from the situation. Leah needed to decide what she wanted, and he couldn't stand by and witness the repercussions if she ended up choosing Bryan over the only way of life they'd ever known.

The only thing left to do was wait...and pray.

* * * *

A few days later, as Leah waited in Nelson's Grocery for Bryan, she removed her bonnet and untied the ribbon binding her hair and let it fall in loose waves around her shoulders. It was a daring move, and something her family would highly disapprove of, but it felt right. She was excited to finally spend a few minutes alone with Bryan, and she wanted to blend in as much as she could with everyone else. There was no telling when her father would approve of her making another delivery alone, so each minute felt precious, and she wanted to make every one of them count.

Bryan appeared from the back room of the store, and when he saw her, he let out a low whistle, which made her blush. "You look beautiful."

She thanked him and as they headed for the door, she felt a shiver race up her spine when he held her hand during their short trek to the coffee shop next door. Several people stopped and stared when they entered the building, but she chose to ignore them. Bryan led her to a small, private corner booth, but instead of sitting across from her, he slid in the booth right beside her, making her heart thump erratically.

A waitress took their order, and they remained there a long time, just talking, drinking coffee and enjoying each other's company. Everything seemed perfect until the topic of discussion turned to money.

"I've been giving it a lot of thought, and I know how you can expand your business," he remarked.

Leah furrowed a brow. "What do you mean?"

His face lit up as he took a pen from his shirt pocket and one of the store napkins and began drawing diagrams while he explained. "You could make a huge profit if you put your business on the internet. We can build a commerce website that's equipped for taking orders, and we could make a fortune."

Leah sat up straight.

"We?" she asked. "Bryan, the people in my community...we don't believe in using things like computers and the internet. I've never had the intention of becoming rich making cheese and selling wool. I do it so I can buy things I need, like shoes and fabric for making dresses."

He seemed genuinely astonished. "But you could be doing so much more. You're just wasting your talent selling it to people here in Walnut Creek."

Hearing him speak so callously about her work and way of life was like someone splashing a bucket of freezing water in her face. He continued explaining how wealthy she could be if she made "the right choices", but Leah distanced herself from him and tuned him out. By the time he had to return to work, she was more than ready to leave. Part of her was heartbroken after witnessing Bryan's true colors, but most of all she was disappointed in herself for acting so foolishly.

Before she left, he made a comment about seeing her again, but as Leah got in her wagon and drove away, she knew without a doubt that would never happen, and she was perfectly okay with it. She tied her hair back and put on her bonnet before heading home, and on the long drive there, she had plenty of time to think about what she wanted and what truly mattered.

When Leah brought the horse and wagon to a stop in her driveway, she saw her father busy plowing the field behind their house, and so she walked hurriedly to the barn, hoping to catch Luke alone so they could talk. She found him storing equipment and preparing to go home.

"If I told you I was wrong, and that I'd been a fool, would you forgive me?"

Luke turned abruptly at the sound of her voice. At first, he seemed excited to see her, but she detected a hint of weariness when he spoke. "Why do you think you've been a fool?"

She walked over to join him, and as she reached for his hands, she was relieved when he didn't object. "Because I chased after something that wasn't meant for me. What God planned for me was right here all along."

He still seemed a bit leery, so Leah did something that surprised them both – she stood on her tiptoes and kissed him. It was a brief kiss, but it had a ripple effect that left them both momentarily speechless.

"I'm still trying to sort all of this out, but I do know I want to give this...*us*...a chance. Am I too late?"

Instead of talking, he answered by pulling her into his embrace and pressing his lips to her own. But this kiss was deeper and more passionate than the first, and when they finally parted, Leah was left breathless and more certain than ever that she'd made the right choice.

This was love. This was where she was meant to be.

AMISH LOVE LETTERS

KATHE CAMPBELL

Chapter One

Golden sheaths of wheat swayed gently in the morning breeze, whispering to each other of lover's secrets and clandestine meetings. The relentless sun beat down from the cornflower blue sky, creating beads of perspiration on the brow of a young, bearded man working in the field. Muscles rippled as his strong shoulders worked tirelessly beneath the simple cheesecloth shirt on his back. He beat the tall stems of the wheat with a long, bladed instrument that spoke of a time gone by. In fact, the young man, whose name was Gael, was Amish. He worked cutting crops in the field, along with his father, and other men from his small community.

As the day wore on, his younger sister Miriam appeared around midday, bearing a woven wicker basket filled with lunch for the men.

"Good afternoon, dearest Brother!" she exclaimed, perpetually happy to see him.

"Hello sister, I do hope you've bought me something delicious for my lunch today?" he replied.

"Don't I always bring you something nice?" she asked, mockingly wounded.

"Of course you do. Come and sit with me whilst I eat". She nodded enthusiastically and skipped ahead of him into a forest glade next to the field, in which the men often sat to eat, taking refuge from the sun in the dappled canopy of the woods. Miriam set her long skirts about her, and sat herself down on a tree root, watching her brother eagerly.

"You'll never guess what happened in the square this morning!?" She said, as soon as Gael was comfortably sitting next to her.

"No, I'll never guess, but I imagine you're going to tell me...?!" he grinned knowingly at her. Miriam, who was 14, had just finished her education and was now learning the skills of her mother and aunts, making bread from the very same wheat that Gael was now harvesting. She was an intelligent young woman with a very keen sense of curiosity, and had immersed herself so completely in the goings on in their village that she was a fountain of knowledge, always bursting to share any new story she had heard. Gael was often the audience of these tales, and although he had little interest in knowing what his neighbor's aunt's cousin bought at the farmer's market, he tried his hardest to listen to his sister's words.

As she chattered away, and Gael sat listening in silence enjoying his lunch, he noticed two women walk into the glade. It was Juliet and Joanne Beauville, two sisters that Gael and Miriam had often played with as children. They came bearing lunch baskets for a large group of men containing their uncles and cousins, and sat down to eat with them. Although he could barely see their faces, which were obscured by the sides of the stiff white bonnets they wore, Gael gazed longingly at the flaxen hair that rippled down the back of Juliet's dress. Though they had spent much time together when they were young, both at school and playing all together with the other children in the village, Gael and Miriam had inevitably drifted apart from the sisters as they entered their teenage years, each following the footsteps of their parents and spending time in the company of those who were to learn the same trade as them. Of course they still saw each other daily, around the village and at church, but it was mostly a customary hello or shy smile. During these years, Gael had admired Juliet from afar, and had developed a strong affection for her. How he longed now, to join the circle where she sat, and strike up a conversation with her about some interesting topic or other. However this was seemingly impossible for Gael, who was extremely shy. To even think about going over there and sitting down next to her, turned his mouth dry, and his palms sweaty. Miriam noticed this.

"Aren't you listening to me?" she demanded.

"Yes of course" he lied, "well no I'm not actually, I'm sorry. My thoughts carried me away"

"What do you mean, what were you thinking about that was more important than listening to me?" she inquired, only half serious.

He hesitated, wondering whether or not to confide in Miriam. He wasn't afraid that she would reveal his secret to anyone else, but it was a secret he carried so close to his heart that he didn't want to tell anyone in the world, not even Juliet herself, for he knew that he would stumble over his words and make a fool of himself, and that everyone would laugh at him. No, he thought, this was a secret he would keep to himself, for now at least.

"Of course, nothing is more important than you, dear sister, please continue." And, mollified, she did.

Later that day, after a delicious meal cooked by their mother Rona, Miriam challenged Gael to a game of scrabble. Their parents sat by the fire, watching and laughing as Miriam constantly disputed her brother's words, but clever though she was, Gael outsmarted her every time. After losing to him a third time, Rona suggested it was time for bed. She helped her children to clear away the game, looking at some of the words on the board as she picked up the tiles.

"You do know some extraordinary words Gael" she chuckled, "but then you've always been like that. You used to write letters to your father and I when you were little, do you remember? We had to look up some of the words you used, I don't know where you learned such big words at that age!"

Gael recalled a memory of sitting at his desk and writing letters containing many pages, to his parents, aunts, uncles and cousins, just for fun. It had always been so much easier for him to express his feelings on paper than to say them out loud, and as a child it had made sense to him to communicate in the way he found most natural. It had been a long time since he had written a letter though. With the complicated emotions of adolescence bubbling away under his shy exterior, he mused that perhaps letter writing was something he should take up again. His thoughts flitted straight to Juliet, and he imagined telling her how he felt, but instead of falling over his words by saying them to her, he imagined putting them eloquently in a letter. The idea swelled within him like a balloon, and by the time he had washed, ready for bed, it had turned into a plan.

Chapter Two

As morning dawned, the rose gold light of the sky seeped through the curtains, and Gael awoke with a start. It had not been long since he had fallen into fitful slumber, having stayed up late into the night to redraft his letter to Juliet countless times. A pile of paper, crunched into balls, lay next to the simple wooden desk he had sat at for many hours, trying to put his feelings into words. Although he had struggled, Gael had consoled himself with the fact that this was, at least, easier than actually saying the words out loud. He was better at writing than at talking, and it was this that might win him the affections of the beautiful Juliet. Gael took the final draft from under his pillow, smoothed out the creases, and reread his letter:

Dear, Sweet, J.

It has taken me many months, months that have turned into years, to write this letter to you. You have floated across my vision every day since we were children, like a rare butterfly, and I have been enchanted by your grace and beauty.

As I labor in the crops, I think of your rose blushed skin, the dimples in your cheeks when you smile, the sapphire blue of your sparkling eyes, and I imagine that one day I would return from the field to a home where it was you who would greet me at the door. When we were young, we would play all day in the brook by your grandmothers house, with your sister and my cousins, chasing each other, laughing freely, and it was then that a seed was planted in my heart. It has grown into a flower that is only fed by the sight of you, or the sound of your sweet voice, or the touch of your hand upon my arm. I would care for you as if you were that delicate and tender bloom, living my whole life to protect you, provide for you and love you.

I can only hope that there is the smallest glimmer of possibility within you that you might permit me to confess my feelings to you, and be inclined to reply to my letter. If that dream may ever become possible, or if only to read the words penned by your hand to spurn me, I hope beyond hope to find your reply, in a secret place where I will hide this letter. I await with a heart full of hope.

> *Yours eternally,*
> *Gael*

Feeling unsure and rather dubious about his entire plan, Gael folded the letter and hastily sealed its envelope before he could change his mind, and quickly got dressed. As he hurried across square, the village was coming to life around him to the sound of a hundred birds singing the dawn chorus. It was going to be a beautiful day, and heartened by this fact, Gael slipped into the barn on the outskirts of the village, that was owned by Juliet's father, and where his wife and daughters worked tending to and milking their cattle and churning butter that was the best in three counties. He had played in the barn countless times with Miriam, Juliet and Joanne. The sisters had shown them the secret hiding space in which they kept items that would be forbidden by their parents. Hoping very much that the space was still used in this manner, Gael crept around the sleepy cows, pushed aside a bale of hay and revealed a small door. On opening it he discovered a crawl space big enough for one person to sit in, and there on the dusty floor was a large tin, filled with chocolate, make up and an old copy of a teen magazine. Smiling, he laid the letter atop the magazine and carefully shut the door.

That evening, Gael returned home exhausted, not from the days work but from the anxiety that had plagued him all day. As he sat down on his bed, a gentle knock came at his door, followed by Miriam's head peeking around.

"Gael my dear, you are a wonderful brother, but a terrible liar! Something is troubling you. I thought you might not want to say in front of Mother and Father, so I didn't press the matter at dinner" she said wisely.

He smiled defeated, "You are too clever for your own good, you know that?"

"It is a heavy burden, but I bear it well" she grinned. "Can I come in?"

"Of course" he replied, and she gently closed the door and took a seat next to him on the bed, her feet dangling an inch or so from the floor. "Well?" she asked.

"Its complicated. Or actually it's quite simple really, but it feels complicated." She looked at him expectantly, she could handle complicated.

"The thing about growing up is that you have to do grown up things, like get married and have children. But sometimes it feels like I'm still a child myself." He turned to see her inquisitive little face gazing up at him.

"You'll be great at that Gael, you are a wonderful brother and you would make a wonderful father and husband. I can't wait to get married!"

"Well I think getting married is the easy part, it's getting there that's the struggle" he said darkly.

She thought for a minute about this, scrunching up her forehead in concentration

"No. I don' think so." She replied. He raised his eyebrows at her. "You just choose who you like best and then you marry them. I'm going to marry Jonah. We already decided that we'll have five children and live on the hill. Who are you going to marry?"

"That" he said, "is a very good question." And with that he scooped her up into his arms and carried her to her own bed, where he wished her sweet dreams and bade her good night. Getting in to his own bed, he marveled at the straight forwardness of Miriam's thinking, and closing his eyes, he pictured Juliet at his side, wearing a white dress and carrying a bouquet of flowers. In a last prayer before sleep, Gael asked for the thing that seemed to him like a miracle. He fell asleep smiling.

<u>Chapter Three</u>

Time moves in a peculiar fashion when you are anticipating something. Gael couldn't decide if he wanted time to slow down so he could put off the eventual moment that he would return to the hiding place of his fate, or if he wanted to find out as quickly as possible, getting the worst over with. Either there would be nothing, an empty space full of meaning, or there would be a letter, containing the words that would determine the rest of his life. Of course, he thought, she might never have found the letter at all, and he wondered what he would do in this case, remove it and pretend it never existed, or leave it and continue the torture that was waiting for her to find it?

The next few days passed in a haze, Gael's mind fully focused on the hiding place, and imagining all sorts of scenarios. He glimpsed Juliet with her sister Joanne several times from afar, but the starched white sides of their bonnets meant that he couldn't see their faces from his angle, making it impossible to see her expression. He wondered if he she had looked at him before he had glanced her way, he felt he had seen both of their heads turn quickly back around as he looked over, but it may well have been his over active imagination.

Finally, the time arrived at which Gael steeled himself to discover the letter, or lack of letter as he was dreading. Rising earlier than usual, he crept once more into the barn, disturbing an owl who had been sleeping there in the rafters. The owl hooted indignantly and flew out of the open door. Gael took a deep breath, and made his way to the back of the barn, moved the hay bale, and opened the small door. He let out a long exhale, having been holding his breath without realizing. There, in the rusty old tin, was a letter with his name on it. Without hesitation, he grabbed the letter and fumbled to open it quickly.

Dear Gael,

I was most shocked but so pleased to read your letter. How sweetly I remember the times playing at grandmother's house, they were my favorite parts of growing up, and I thought of you so fondly then. Having always been so quiet it was quite impossible to tell of your affection towards me, but I am full of happiness to learn of it. I have always felt apart from the other girls, their talk can often be dreary and I find myself drifting apart from them. I could see that you were different too, even though we have drifted apart since becoming older, I see a sensitivity, and a wisdom in you that is rare in so many of the men in our village. Your words were full of a beautiful poetry that moved me, and I confess to feeling you in my heart as well. I hope you will continue to write me, I have seen a different side of you in your letter and I desire to know the mind of the man behind those shy eyes of yours. Waiting for your reply with much anticipation,

> *Your J. x*

Feeling his heart lift, and a warm tingling sensation extending all over his body, as though the sun was shining on his bare skin, an enormous weight lifted off Gael's shoulders, floating away into nothingness as dream became reality. He sat and reread the letter several times, before remembering that he would be missed at work. Walking across the square with a spring in his step, it felt almost as though he was in somebody else's body, the unfamiliar feeling of confidence coursed through his veins and breathed new life into his very soul.

"What do you look so happy about?" demanded Miriam, as Gael joined her at the table for breakfast.

"It's just a beautiful day, isn't it?"

"If you say so" she replied, eyeing him suspiciously.

Everything seemed brighter that day. The birds sang sweetly, the gentle breeze ruffled his hair and cooled his skin in the midday heat. The flower in his heart had opened to full bloom, turning it's petals outwards toward the sun, full of a divine nectar that filled his insides with a warm, golden glow. Gael itched to get home and begin writing his reply, he tried to construct the sentences in his head but was too giddy with happiness to order his thoughts properly; it would be easier when he put them on paper.

Miriam came at lunchtime again, and they took their usual spot on the edge of the glade. Gael ate in silence, without even the pretense of listening to Miriam's chatter. Far over the other side of the wooded spot, Juliet and Joanne walked to a group of men, arm in arm, carrying their baskets. They were too far away to read their faces, but Gael was sure that they had looked in his direction and giggled to each other. He took this as a good sign. As they sat in the circle of brothers, cousins, father and uncles, with their backs to him, Gael felt a strange desire to go and join the same circle. He kept half an eye on that corner of the glade as he finished his food, and was surprised to see the two sisters get up from the circle and head over his way. His heart leapt into his mouth and suddenly his palms began to sweat. The familiar sensations of anxiety crept upon him, and he looked helplessly at Miriam, who has stopped talking and was watching her brother.

"Hi Miriam, Hi Gael!" chimed Juliet and her sister as one, both beaming at the pair as they walked past.

"Hello!" greeted Miriam, catching Gael's eye out of the corner of her own. "Beautiful day isn't it?!" she grinned, and in that instant Gael knew that she knew.

Chapter Four

Sat at his desk that evening, his pencil and paper before him, Gael began to write in earnest.

Dear, sweet, J.

My heart is singing with the song of a thousand angels. Gott has truly smiled upon me this day, for I have never been happier than to read your delightful letter. Every word was a honeyed treat, a delicious indulgence that filled me with a heavenly gratification.

To see you this afternoon, to hear your melodic voice, if only for a second, was sustenance for a man starved. Can it be possible that you are more charming than I ever even imagined? The sun shines a light that illuminates you and dulls all others in your wake. Your skin glittered with the radiance of dappled sunbeams in that glade, your smile is a new day dawning. I could praise you until the day I die, and on that day I would die a happy man for being given the greatest pleasure on earth, to have looked upon you every day and basked in the glow of your beauty and greatness.

We have shared church, classroom, playground and village for our entire lives, and I consider myself lucky to have known you in that time. But I confess myself longing to know you better, to know your entirety, every fiber of your being. What drives you, what are your dreams and fears, what thoughts occur in that beautiful brain of yours?! I long to know you sweet girl, I hope you'll share with me all that you are.

Yours,

Gael

Consumed with a love like he had never known before, Gael waited in a state of high anticipation for her response. He took to checking the secret hiding place in the barn every day, although he did not have to wait long for his reply.

Dear Gael,

You are most kind to shower me with such compliments, and a smile plays on my lips to read your exultations. Yet I admit to being perplexed, your writing is that of a confident and strong minded man, and yet when we meet face to face, you seem lost and withdrawn. I struggle to put the man on paper to the face of that who I see every day, and who I have known since childhood. What drives me? A love of Gott, above all else, and a willingness to do His bidding until time immemorial. My dreams and fears propel me as one, for although our Order discourages education beyond the years of our early teens, I have harbored a secret desire to continue learning, something that I can confess only to you. Such is your open and candid way that I feel I can tell you anything in confidence. The tin in which we have been hiding our letters, contains a hidden bottom, and it is in here that I conceal the books that I have taken from the public library, without the knowledge of my parents. I hide them even in the most secret of hiding places, as my sister shares this place with me, it is her makeup and magazines that you see, and she would judge me mightily if she knew my secrets. I fear that she would tell our parents and they would have me excommunicated, a thought that I cannot bear to entertain, for the community means everything to me. I hope you will not misunderstand my intentions, I do not wish to shun the order, the church, or the Lord Himself. But I cannot close my eyes to the world outside; I want to possess knowledge of all that is possible to learn. I will pray, with much hope that you understand.

Your J.x

Gael folded the letter and sat down on the bale of hay that concealed the secret door. It was a lot to take in. Disobeying the rules of Amish tradition was a dangerous thing to do. He never would have thought it of her, and yet the feeling he had was not one of foreboding, but of great admiration. This was a side to her that he could never have anticipated, and one that was mirrored deep within him. He had regretted that his education had ended to make way for learning the skills his father would teach him, tending to the crops and harvesting the wheat. It was tradition ingrained so profoundly deep that it never occurred to the majority of Amish that there was any other path. But Gael had always had a strong sense of curiosity, and a thirst for knowledge that was not satiated by the Bible alone. He had not gone so far as Juliet, to take books that were not prohibited in his society, and hide them from even his closest family, but he had felt a desire to rebel against the path laid out for him before. Although he knew he shouldn't endorse this behavior, he felt pride at the courage it took for his beloved to chase her dreams regardless at the potential impact it could have on her entire life.

Chapter Five

Since the day that he had found the first letter in the barn, Gael looked as though he had grown an extra few inches. He hadn't, of course, but the confidence within himself had caused him to walk, stand and even act differently, with more purpose and meaning in every step. It was a palpable change, and his whole family noticed it. Gael, however, was unaware that his family was giving him knowing smiles; he was too lost in his thoughts of the girl he had always dreamed of, for now his dream had come true.

After the last letter, in which Juliet professed her darkest secret to him, Gael had written his shortest reply yet:

J,

I understand, and I love you all the more for it. I have seen a different side to you that has enraptured me even more, a feat I never thought possible. Will you meet me tomorrow night, in the barn? Your written words are no longer enough, I wish to look upon your face as I confess my feelings.

Gael

The next morning, Gael woke with butterflies in his stomach, and it took him a few seconds to realize why. He could not wait to finally be united with the woman he loved. It was hard for him to believe that it was happening, after all the years he had secretly harbored feelings for her, tonight was the night. He dressed particularly carefully, and made his way down to join his family for breakfast.

"Gael, don't forget that tonight is the horse show and I'll need your help at the auction over in Lancaster.' said Gael's father, Merle.

With a shock of horror, Gael realized his mistake. In all his concentration on writing love letters, he had forgotten his promise to help out his father, a job that would require him to work into the early hours, and therefore miss his meeting with Juliet.

"You forgot didn't you?" Merle asked with disappointment. "You promised me weeks ago that you could help; otherwise I would have asked your cousins!"

"I'm sorry Father, I did forget, but its fine, I'll still help you, I'll come to Lancaster with you."

Fretfully, Gael wondered how it would be possible to tell Juliet in time that he had to rearrange their rendezvous.

"Miriam can you please hurry and finish your breakfast, I need you to run this dish over to the Beauville's before school" said their mother as she bustled into the kitchen. Seizing the opportunity, Gael jumped up and took the dish from his mother's hands.

"I'll take it for you, I'm leaving now anyway." And he dashed to the door, barely registering Miriam's knowing look as he left the house.

Striding across the square towards Juliet's house, he was surprised at his lack of anxiety. The only thing that mattered to him was making sure he could inform her of his change of plans. It would be awful to think of her there waiting for him, not knowing that he wouldn't come.

He rapped on the door, which was opened almost immediately by Juliet's sister Joanne. She looked surprised to see him, but quickly broke into a huge grin.

"Couldn't you wait until this evening?" she asked playfully. Gael hesitated; Juliet must have told her about their correspondence.

"I just, my mother asked me to return this dish..." She took it from him, purposefully brushing his hand with hers.

"I can't wait until tonight" she whispered, and flashing him one more smile, she turned with the dish, and closed the door.

Gael stood dumbstruck on the step for a minute, completely confused at the exchange. He ambled slowly back across the square and was well into the field before realization slowly dawned on him. Joanne had read the letters meant for Juliet. He felt numb at the monumental mistake, and wondered how he could have been so stupid. He marked the letters with the initial they both shared, used the hiding place they had shown him together, and both used now even as adults. And although everything seemed wrong, the facts began to slide neatly into place. Joanne, the eldest sister, had excelled at school. She was witty and intelligent as a child, and somehow slightly more abrasive than her coy younger sister because of it. The two sisters had thrown him glances, but it was Joanne that was smiling back his way, only he had missed it because he was staring at Juliet. He supposed it made sense that she thought his letters were for her, when they had played together as children they had been the ringleaders as the eldest of their playmates.

Gael was heavily embarrassed. He had been so foolish to think that Juliet had loved him in return, and with this thought all of his old insecurities came rushing back. How could he possibly explain the mix up to the sisters? He knew Joanne would go to the barn tonight, and he wouldn't be there. Would it be possible to explain what had happened? Would he still have a chance with Juliet after he had misled her sister? He knew they were close and Joanne was likely to have shared this with her. Gael had no doubt that trying to rectify the whole mess would be complicated, and saw no real conclusion in which he was likely to come out winning. Time was running out, there were only a few short hours in which to make some very difficult decisions. Was it possible that he could explain his mistake to Joanne and not let his father down?

Like clockwork, Miriam arrived with Gael's lunch. She could tell straight away that he was in turmoil.

"Gael, what's wrong, you look terrible?!"

"I've made a huge mistake" he replied glumly.

"It's Joanne, isn't it? I know you've liked her for ages. Has something happened?"

He stared at her. "Joanne?"

"Yes, Joanne!" she said, somewhat exasperated, "Don't try and act dumb, I know you two have something going on. Tell me!"

"But..." he trailed off. "Joanne?" he mused, and somehow, everything became clear to him, as though his heart had been covering his true feelings, and was now revealing them like the grand trick at the end of the magicians performance.

"Miriam, I need your help. I haven't got much time. Can you do something for me? It's about Joanne."

She looked absolutely delighted to be included in her dear brother's secrets, and equally smug about being right, although she had little idea how right she really was.

"Of course" she answered her brother, leaning forward conspiratorially. "What's the plan?".

<u>Chapter Six</u>

The buggy ride to Lancaster was over two hours long, and Gael spent the journey agonizing over all that had happened, wondering how it was possible that his feeling had sneakily crept up behind him and jumped out, as if shouting "Surprise!" However, he felt the sort of lightness that comes with knowing a truth about oneself, it had been unknowingly bubbling away beneath the surface. All that was left to resolve was finally seeing Joanne face to face, admitting his feelings to her now he had finally admitted them to himself.

The auction was a success, Gael and his father sold a considerable amount of the horses they bred, and it was with high spirits that they began the journey back to their village, the full moon bright in the cloudless sky. Gael observed his father, and hoped that he could one day be the sort of man Merle was, a strong man, a good husband, and a devoted father. He saw a future with Joanne stretching out in front of him, like rolling hills and valleys, a beautiful adventure that they would embark on together. His heart soared with the idea of it, and as they rounded the corner on to the final approach, Gael was filled with excitement.

On sight of the village however, Gael's heart fell all the way into the pit of his stomach, for great big billowing furls of black smoke ascended from the distance, a burning orange glow beneath it.

"Fire!" exclaimed Merle, with a sharp intake of breath, "But where?" He gee'd up the horses and they sped closer to the blaze. "It looks like the Beauville's barn!"

Gael blanched, he knew it was true, the barn coming into sight as they arrived in the square. Leaping down before the buggy had come to a halt, he raced to the barn, ignoring the cries of his father. As the burning building came into view, he saw a crowd of people outside, with some men trying to beat back the flames at the barn door, women and children rushing back and forth with various containers filled with water. Juliet was among them, and as she saw Gael, she cried out "Joanne is in there! She went to meet you and never came back!" tears streamed down her face as she looked hopelessly at Gael. He joined the men closest to the door and saw that there was no way of getting in. Hopelessness began to engulf him, and images of Joanne crossed his mind; Joanne bringing lunch to the glade, Joanne playing with her sister as a child, Joanne hiding books in her secret hiding place...

With a jolt like lightening, Gael realized what to do. In seconds he had arrived at the other side of the barn. He sized up quickly where he thought the compartment might join the outer wall. Hoping against hope, he grabbed a rusty scythe and started to smash the lowest planks of the wooden wall. He heard a faint scream, "Help! I'm in here!" It was Joanne. Her voice spurred him to work faster, demolishing the only thing that stood between him and his beloved. After a few more minutes, he could see a pale hand reach through the gap he had created. Carefully removing a few more planks, he grabbed the hand and pulled. Joanne emerged from the hole, her face and dress blackened from the smoke. He gathered her into his big arms and rushed back around to the front of the barn. Juliet shrieked in relief, and pulled the local doctor towards Gael and her sister. As he set Joanne down to be examined, a sobbing Miriam ran over to him.

"Gael", she cried, "I'm so sorry, it all went wrong, I went there, to the barn, but I couldn't see Joanne and I was looking around and I dropped the lantern and...and..." she dissolved into further tears and buried her face in her hands, completely distraught. Gael took her hands so he could look into her tearful eyes.

"It's OK, it's not your fault, it was an accident. Joanne will be fine. Please don't cry!" But she couldn't stop, so he grabbed her into a big hug, and didn't let go.

Meanwhile, the villagers had managed control the fire. From where he stood, Gael could see that the main structure of the barn remained intact, it was the door which had caught fire, and luckily it had not spread to the hay bales of the cattle.

"Look, it's not so bad" he tried to comfort his sister.

Taking great, heaving breaths, she replied "I ran and told what had happened straight away."

Beside them, the doctor stood Joanne up and told them "She'll be fine, it's just a little smoke inhalation. It sounds like hiding in that concealed space kept out most of the smoke.

Joanne turned to face Gael, and he let go of Miriam who went to stand with Juliet.

"Well you are quite the hero. You saved my life!" said Joanne to Gael, a smile playing on her lips.

"I'd do anything for you" he told her, his expression serious. "I'm sorry I wasn't there tonight. I've made a bit of a mess of things lately, but you're OK and that's all that matters. I love you Joanne, every part of you. And I always will." And then he cupped his hands around her dirt streaked face, and kissed her tenderly.

"It's a good start" she smiled back at him as he broke away to look deep into her eyes. Gael suddenly realized that everyone around him was watching them, and had started clapping and cheering.

"I guess the secret is out" he said, smiling back at Joanne. Then he took her into his arms once more, and kissed her so passionately that she knew she would spend the rest of her life loving him, and being loved in return.

AMISH SHY

DEIDRA SCOTT

Chapter One

Abe Miller took a deep breath of the fresh spring air and smiled. There was nothing quite like the smell of early April air on an Amish farm. Bending down, Abe took a handful of the dark dirt he had just been plowed and rolled it around between his fingers. Damp and moist, the rich soil promised to be the perfect spot for a garden.

"Abe, Abe!" From his spot in the field, Abe could hear his mother's voice calling him from the house.

Wiping his hands off on his black pants legs, Abe started toward the house, anxious to see what his mother had to say.

At twenty-four, Abe was one of the oldest unmarried men in his Amish community. All of his six brothers and sisters had already moved away from home and started families of their own. While Abe had planned to have a wife long before now, his *daed*'s death had put a halt to his plans. Rather than pursue a girlfriend, Abe had chosen to stop attending gatherings of the young people and instead focused entirely on helping his *mamm*. There had been so many bills and so much work to be done, that Abe had put his all into working on a construction crew during the day and putting in long hours on the farm when he got home at night. Now, four years later, Abe was beginning to see the pay-off for all his hours of hard work. The mortgage on the farm was closed to being paid and, for once, the animals had actually started to make more money than they cost.

Life was truly starting to look up. Soon, Abe would be able to quit his construction work and devote all his time to the farm. With nothing to focus on except developing the farm, he had faith that he would be able to make it a great success. Abe had hopes of one day expanding their acreage so that they could plant several crops, mow hay to sell, and raise large amounts of animals.

There was only one thing that nagged at Abe's mind, and that was the thought of Rebecca Graber. Before his dad passed away, Abe and Rebecca had enjoyed spending time together at young peoples' events and had even been what many people considered a couple. But that had all disappeared after Mr. Miller died. Abe had been forced to turn away from Rebecca and what was beginning to look like a possible relationship was nipped in the bud.

Shaking his head, Abe took a deep breath. There was no reason to think of Rebecca. It had been years since they had even spoken. Despite the fact that she was as beautiful as ever, Abe realized that there was no hope for a future with her now. He had closed off that possibility when he turned away from her so many years ago.

As he got closer to the house, Abe could see a row of black buggies ties close to the porch.

"*Ach*, why would they be here?" He wondered to himself as he recognized the buggies as belonging to the church board. Goodness knew Abe couldn't have done anything to receive a scolding from the church; it had been years since he'd even had energy enough to step a foot outside of the rules set forward by his community.

Stepping through the back door, Abe quickly rinsed his hands in the washbasin and then hurried into the front room. Mrs. Miller was bustling around the kitchen, working to prepare a pot of tea to offer her guests. Gathered around the large wooden table was the entire church board.

"Hello," Abe said awkwardly as he gave a nod toward the group of men.

Sam Swartz rose to his feet and nodded back, "Morning, Abe. Take a seat. We've something to talk to you about."

Abe took a deep breath and sat down at the head of the kitchen table, nervous about what might be coming next.

"Well, Abe, I don't want to beat around the bush for too long," Sam finally announced, "We're here on business. As you've probably realized, our community is in sore need of a preacher. Josiah Eicher is getting ready to move away to Kentucky and we need someone to replace him."

Abe raised his eyebrows, "I know that. Josiah's been a *gut* friend over the years, but what does this have to do with me?"

Sam looked toward the other men at the table. Several of them nodded their heads and another spoke up to say, "Go on, Sam. Just tell him."

Sam bit his lips together and then looked at Abe uncertainly, "We used to draw lots to choose new preachers like the other Amish communities...but this time we've decided to do something different. Everybody around here is so busy trying to take care of their farms and provide for their families...there isn't a single Amish man who feels like he can take on the job."

"I can't blame them," Abe spoke up, "It's a big responsibility."

"Abe," it was now Hiram Yoder's turn to talk, "You know the Amish way is to get married and raise a family. That's what we believe God has put us on this earth to do. While we realize that you have been a *gut* man for taking care of your mom during her time of trouble after your dad died, you've become selfish over the years. You are so focused on getting more and more, that you've forgotten the important things. We know you're succeeding...but now it's time to step back and devote some time to the Lord."

"We've decided you are to be the next preacher," Sam announced boldly, totally interrupting Hiram's more gentle approach.

Abe felt his mouth drop open and he immediately started shaking his head, "No, no, you can't mean that." He tried to protest, "I don't accept the job."

"Abe," Hiram smiled softly as he rose from his seat, "You don't understand, this isn't an offer...it is what you are going to do."

Abe watched as the church board all stood up from their places at the table. He felt desperate to stop them, "You don't understand! I am no good as a preacher...I have no skills at all. My ability to speak in public is non-existent!"

One of the men gave him a pat on the shoulder and Sam announced, "The Lord will provide what you need."

With that, they were gone, leaving Abe alone with his grim new job.

Chapter Two

Rebecca Graber smiled softly as listened to Leah Yoder talking on and on about how big her new baby cousin was. Sitting around the large quilt frame, the group of women usually found that their mouths went a lot faster than their fingers. Although gossiping was forbidden among the Amish, it was difficult for the women to get together without sharing a lot of interesting talk from the community.

"Josiah Eicher's family has set a moving date," one of the women announced as she reached up to adjust her bonnet, "Wednesday afternoon."

"*Ach*," another woman spoke up, "I hate to see them go. Josiah's been one of the best preachers we've ever had. Who will fill his shoes?"

Rebecca found her thoughts traveling to something else as she studied a piece of the flowered fabric in her hand.

"Haven't you heard the news?" Suzie Bontrager asked, "The board got together and hand-picked a new preacher!"

Rebecca raised an eyebrow as she absent-mindedly listened. She had never known of the community to pick their own preacher.

"Who?" Someone asked with excitement.

"Why, it's Abe Miller!" Suzie exclaimed.

The words brought Rebecca from her thoughts about planting flowers that looked like those on the quilt square. Rebecca looked up in surprise and suddenly found her fingers feeling weak as she tried to work.

"Surely not!" One of the other women said with a gasp, "Abe has hardly spoken a word to anyone since his *daed* died. He wasn't very talkative before that, either, but his dad's death changed him completely."

The words were true. Abe had never been one to talk up a storm, but Rebecca could remember times when they had sat together at the young peoples' events and their conversation had come easily.

Rebecca found herself feeling instantly self-conscious and wishing that she could just go home.

"Rebecca," The sound of her name coming from Suzie's lips made Rebecca feel almost sick, "Didn't you and Abe go out together when you were teenagers?"

Rebecca forced herself to nod her head slowly.

"Then I'd say you know him better than anyone," Laura Schmidt announced, "Goodness knows that Abe hasn't said more than boo to anyone in the last four years."

Rebecca knew that better than anyone. She had spent each day, hoping that Abe would come back into her life. It felt like her heart had broken a little bit more each week that he avoided the young peoples' gatherings and ignored her when he saw her at church.

"What is he like, Rebecca?" Suzie asked as she stabbed her needle back into the fabric, "Do you think he'll make a good preacher?"

Rebecca took a deep breath and reached up to brush a strand of dark blonde hair away from her eyes, "It's been so long, I hardly remember what he's like. *Ach*, but goodness, we were hardly more than just friends."

Several of the women looked at each other and raised their eyebrows.

Rebecca found herself ducking her head, trying to avoid their prying eyes. To say they were just friends was ridiculous. She was sure everyone already wondered why, at twenty-two she hadn't found herself a steady beau yet. Over the years, she had courted many of the young men in her community, yet nothing had ever been serious enough for her to move forward with a relationship.

Recently, Rebecca had started cleaning house for the Amish widower Simon Girod. While Rebecca couldn't say that she felt very close to Simon, it was beginning to look like he was her only hope of every having a family of her own.

Silently, Rebecca found herself regretting ever having spoken to Abe Miller. She wished that she could go back in time and she would never have returned his attention. One thing was certain: Rebecca wouldn't be letting herself make that mistake again, even if Abe was to beg her.

Abe Miller carefully hammered a board in place on Mrs. Simms' new back porch. For the last week, he and the work crew had been crafting a wooden platform behind the Simms house.

Abe found himself taking out his frustration on the nail as he drove it deep into the wooden plank.

For the past four years, Abe had grown accustomed to doing the same thing every day. He got up early in the morning, cared for the animals, went with the work crew and did construction jobs until afternoon, then he went back home to finish more farm chores. By the time night came, Abe would be so exhausted, he could think of nothing but going to bed.

Now, he found himself overwhelmed with other, unwanted thoughts. In a little over a four days time, Abe would be standing in front of the entire Amish community, delivering a sermon. He had no idea what he was going to say or if he would even have the ability to open his mouth and form words.

And if Hiram Yoder hadn't brought up the fact that Abe wasn't married. That alone had filled Abe's thoughts and dreams with memories of Rebecca Miller.

It had been four years since they had spoken. Abe could still remember the night that she attended his *daed's* viewing. She had come over to try to comfort him, but Abe had pushed her away. He had felt like he was unable to have both a girlfriend and provide for his family. It had been more than Abe could do alone, so he had ended things. He hadn't done it very kindly; instead, he simply told her it was over...for her to go on with her life.

Abe wished that he had done something differently, but he wasn't sure what. Surely it was better to end things quickly than to try to hold it all together and watch it fall apart.

Pounding another board in place, Abe found himself hoping he could find some way to get out of this new job as a preacher. This job was certainly beyond his capabilities, and the urge to quite before he made a fool of himself was overwhelming.

"We should be finished with this project today," Abe heard his boss, Levi Christner announce, "Next up is refinishing one of the rooms in widower Sam Girod's house."

Abe took a deep breath. Hopefully he could get lost in his work and forget what was ahead of him.

Chapter Three

Rebecca Miller grabbed her shawl and straightened her prayer cap. She stood at the window, waiting for her driver to arrive. It was Thursday and Sam Girod had asked Rebecca to come clean his house.

Rebecca took a deep breath and shook her head. Sam was a lonely thirty-five-year-old widower with no children of his own. While Sam had shown no interest in her yet, Rebecca's mother was pushing her to take advantage of this opportunity and try to convince Sam that she would be a good wife.

Just the idea made Rebecca feel sick to her stomach, but she realized that she was getting older and her opportunities to get a boyfriend were starting to dwindle fast. Getting married and raising children was the Amish way; without that, what purpose would Rebecca's life have?

When Rebecca arrived at Sam's house, she was surprised to find a truck parked outside the front door.

"*Ach*, would could be here?" She wondered to herself as she handed her driver some money and hurried inside to get started.

Sam owned a small store in town and spent most of his time at it, leaving Rebecca alone to clean most of the day. Seeing an *Englisher's* vehicle there made her nervous.

Stepping into the house, Rebecca heard the sound of hammers pounding in the back room.

Turning a corner, looking for Sam and anxious to see what was going on, Rebecca walked right into Abe Miller. Taking a step backward, Rebecca thought she might lose her balance. On instinct, Abe reached out and grabbed for her shoulder, trying to steady her.

"Abe," Rebecca regained her footing and found herself looking directly into his green eyes, "I certainly didn't expect to see you here." Suddenly bashful, she looked down at the floor.

"Sam hired us to come work on that back bedroom." Abe explained, stepping back from Rebecca and playing absent-mindedly with the hammer on his tool belt.

"Oh, Rebecca, you're here." Sam announced as he appeared from the back room, "I'm sorry I didn't warn you about all this work going on. As you pointed out, rain has been leaking in that back bedroom and has destroyed a place on the floor. Plus, there is now some black mold growing on the ceiling and down the wall. The crew is going to repair it all this week."

The idea of being stuck in a house with Abe wasn't Rebecca's cup of tea.

"Would you want me to go home and come back another day?" Rebecca was quick to ask.

Sam shook his head, "Oh, no! I told them to keep the mess back there. Go on and clean what you can. With them working like this, I may actually need you to come more often."

Rebecca glanced at Abe, almost asking for his approval to stay. She felt so wrong to be there, so close to the man who had ended their relationship so abruptly.

"Well, I'm off to work," Sam announced, "Rebecca, I left you some money on the table for cleaning."

With that, Sam was gone, leaving Rebecca and Abe alone in the hallway.

"I'll try to stay out of your way." Rebecca announced coldly.

Abe gave a nod, "I'll do the same."

As if his new job as a preacher wasn't enough for Abe to worry about, having Rebecca in the same house nearly drove him insane.

While he wanted to avoid her, Abe also found himself anxious to catch another glimpse of her.

She was still so beautiful. Looking into her blue eyes had taken Abe back four years. He found himself lost in memories of the time that they had spent together. And Abe found himself overwhelmed with guilt about the way that he had unexpectedly broken things off.

By the time he got home that night, Abe felt almost sick to his stomach. Once his barn chores were over, he went to his room and sat down at his wooden desk. Grabbing a piece of paper and a pen, Abe tried to decide what he was going to preach about. Flipping his Bible open, he searched for a story that might be appropriate.

He wondered if he could simply give up, preach the worst sermon of all times, and then enjoy being fired.

Abe found himself unable to think of anything but Rebecca. He had done her wrong. He knew it now and he had even known it four years ago.

"Knock, knock!" Abe heard his mother's cheerful voice outside his bedroom door.

"Come in, Mom," He said with a deep sigh.

"You look exhausted," his mother announced as she stepped into his bedroom, "Hard day?"

Abe slowly nodded his head, "I guess you could say that." He was silent for a moment, trying to decide how much he should share with his mother, "Mom, I just feel like the church is expecting too much of me."

Mrs. Miller smiled as she sat on the edge of her son's bed and reached down to smooth out the quilt that she had made him years ago, "Son, you've always been one to put your mind to something and do it."

Abe rested his forehead on the palm of his hand, "I think this is just more than I can handle. You know I'm no good at talking to large groups of people. I stutter and stumble and can't get two words to come out right. This is going to be nothing short of a disaster!"

"Abe, you've always been one to plow ahead and do whatever you want, but you also shy away from anything you might fail trying."

Abe let out a laugh, "I think that's probably natural, Mama."

Chucking to herself, Mrs. Miller announced, "I'm sure you're right on that one, but life is full of challenges. That's one of the greatest blessings of the Lord...He promises to give us the strength to do the things we couldn't do on our own. Where we are weak, He is very strong. He'll help you get through this, Abe...if you let Him."

Abe knew that his mother's words were true. She knew her Bible better than anyone, but those words were much easier to know in his heart than to actually act on.

"If you read that Bible," Mrs. Miller told him, standing up and reaching out to pat him on the back, "You'll find a lot of people who did big things...and the Lord helped them each. Without Him they would have been nothing, but with Him, they couldn't fail. If you ask God to help you and do what He tells you to do, you're going to succeed." Reach out to the door, she whispered, "*Gut* night, son."

"Goodnight, *Mamm*," he muttered back, watching as she stepped out into the hallway and closed the door behind her.

From the time he had been a little boy, Abe had been overwhelmed by so many different fears. Some of the things he shied away from doing were certainly for the best, but he had also made terrible decisions in an effort to keep from doing something he felt was beyond his own capabilities.

Rebecca Graber had been one of those choices. When life seemed too hard, he had simply jilted her; tossed her aside as if her feelings didn't matter. Just the thought of it made Abe's heart feel weighed down by guilt. There was nothing he could do to right his wrongs now, was there?

Closing his eyes, Abe gripped his Bible tightly between his hands.

"Lord," he prayed softly, "I don't know why you let the church elders pick me as their new preacher. Surely, I'm as ill-fit for the job as anyone on the earth. I'm no public speaker and I don't even know how I'm going to write a sermon, let alone speak it in front of all the community. I need your help. You surely gave me this job, Lord. Please, either get me out of it or help me do it. I don't want to run away anymore."

Chapter Four

For the first time in years, Rebecca found herself crying into her pillow that Thursday night. Lying in bed, she tried to keep her sobs to herself so as not to wake her younger sister, Sadie, who was sleeping in the same room.

Obviously, her efforts were futile.

"Are ya all right, sister?" Sadie whispered into the darkness, sitting up in bed when Rebecca couldn't hold in an especially large sob.

"I'm fine," Rebecca tried to sound normal, but she couldn't hide the quiver in her voice.

"You're not fine," Eighteen-year-old Sadie insisted as she got up and moved to sit on the edge of Rebecca's bed, "What's wrong?"

Rebecca shook her head, struggling to make out her sister's concerned expression in the light of the moon.

"When I went to clean Sam's house today..." Rebecca took a deep breath, willing herself to calm down as she whispered the news to her sister, "I went around a corner and ran right into none other than Abe Miller himself. I ran full force into him, Sadie. I almost fell over...probably would have if he hadn't reached out to grab me."

"Humph," Sadie let out a snort, "If I was you, I would have smacked him but good! New preacher or not, I haven't forgiven him for all that happened back when you two were courting."

The idea of smacking the new preacher almost caused Rebecca to laugh, but instead she just sighed, "I hate to admit it, Sadie, but I still have feelings for him. He's working at Sam's right now. Here I went to work this morning, planning to try to win Sam's heart...and I found my own all tangled up in Abe Miller. I kept peeking around the corners, hoping I'd see him again."

Sadie raised an eyebrow, "I'd be hoping to see him so my broom handle could 'accidentally' slap him right upside the head."

When Sadie saw that she would not be able to make her older sister laugh, she cautiously said, "I never knew what happened between you two. One day you were happy together and he was taking you places, and the next he was gone."

Rebecca nodded and whispered softly, "That's about how it went for me, too. I never knew what happened. Like you said, one day things were going good. We would go together to the young peoples' gatherings – I would feel so safe and happy sitting there by his side on his buggy. Then his *daed* died...and everything changed. I went to the viewing, hoping to talk to him." Rebecca closed her eyes at the memory, "I was just saying regular things about how sorry I was...when, suddenly, he announced that he had to help his *mamm* and would be staying busy, so I would need to find someone else to drive me. He said I needed to just go on with my life and forget him. He seemed so resigned and indifferent about the entire situation. I spent every night, hoping that he would eventually come back around, but he didn't. With that, everything ended. When I saw him places, he was like a stranger."

"Well," Sadie's tone had softened, "His dad's death was unexpected and there was a lot of work to do..."

"I thought the same at first," Rebecca agreed, "But, *ach*, Sadie, it's been four years. I can only think that he never loved me at all and his dad's death was just an excuse to end things."

"Well," Sadie started again, "if that's the case, then I think you should've hit him good with the broom handle! Leah, if he's a man like that, then he doesn't deserve your tears. Think of Sam...he's a *gut* man. Don't be spending all your time crying over a loser; instead, think about what you could have with Sam."

Rebecca wiped her eyes and nodded her head. She would think of Sam, and put Abe Miller far away from her thoughts.

Abe lay in bed. Despite the fact that he was exhausted, he couldn't sleep. Something about his prayer had relieved some of his fears, but made him even more nervous in other ways.

No matter what he did, he couldn't help but think of Rebecca. It seemed that she now invaded his thoughts more than ever.

Over and over, his mind replayed the night that they broke up. Abe knew that he had treated her wrong. His conscience whispered that it was time to make things right, but his mind assured him that was a bad idea.

Ach, hadn't he heard that Rebecca had a boyfriend now? Wasn't it rumored that she and Sam Girod had something going on? Chances were, she didn't care about Abe at all anymore. Maybe she didn't even remember that they had ever courted. Going to talk to her now would be ridiculous.

You'll be making a fool of yourself, Abe Miller!

But, on the other hand, he had treated her badly. He had been harsh and cold, and Abe found himself regretting every choice he had made after his *daed* did.

He still loved her. Abe realized that the moment that she had stepped right into him that very morning. She had been so close. Reaching out to grab her shoulder had been as much a pleasure for him as it was an attempt to keep her on her feet.

Taking a deep breath, Abe rolled over in bed and closed his eyes.

"I'll talk to her if you want, God," he prayed into the darkness, "But you'd better be with me, because this sure won't be easy!"

Chapter Five

Rebecca was busy washing laundry on the back porch with Sadie that bright Saturday morning. For the first time in days, she felt as if she might be able to get past seeing Abe at Sam's house. Now, if she could just make it through the Sunday morning service, she could forget about his existence for the next two weeks.

"Rebecca," she heard her mom call from inside the house, "Abe Miller is here to see you."

Instantly, Rebecca's sunny disposition fell. She could hardly believe her ears.

She looked at her sister whose mouth was hanging open in surprise.

"Well," Sadie announced when she finally got past the initial shock, "I suppose you must have made some sort of an impact on him the other morning."

Abe paced the Graber's kitchen floor uncomfortably as he waited on Rebecca to appear.

"Would you like a cookie?" Mrs. Graber offered him a plate of fresh-baked chocolate chip cookies.

Abe instinctively took one off the plate, but couldn't bring himself to eat it. Instead, he just stood with it in his hand, unsure what to do next.

Suddenly, Rebecca appeared from the backroom. Her expression was stern and her face almost ashen.

Abe wondered if he had lost his mind completely. Surely, Rebecca didn't even remember their time together after all these years and, if she did, she certainly didn't think about it now.

"Preacher," she announced calmly, "What a surprise."

Abe winced at her words, but forced himself to plow ahead, "Would you like to step outside and talk for a few minutes?"

Rebecca gave something close to a nod and followed him onto the front porch.

"Rebecca," Abe took a deep breath, "It's been so many years...I...well..." Abe closed his eyes, suddenly wondering if his Sunday message would go something like this.

"Rebecca," he tried again, "I've come to tell you that I'm sorry."

"Sorry for what?"

"Years ago, we used to...we went places together. Do you remember that?"

Rebecca stared straight at him, her expression completely blank, "I remember something about it, yes."

"After my *daed* did," Abe looked down at his feet, "Everything changed. I wasn't a good friend, Rebecca. In fact, I was a terrible person all the way around. I feel so uncertain of everything. I had so much responsibility piled in my lap and it seemed like I wouldn't be able to do it all. My *mamm* showed me the bills, and it looked like I would spend the rest of my life working. The mortgage...and just the general bills to pay for my family...*daed* was a good man, but he left us nothing but bills. I was so scared, but I knew that I could work if I put my mind to it. I buckled down and chose to throw aside everything to just focus on working. I didn't think I could handle more than one thing at a time."

Rebecca said nothing, and Abe found himself shifting from one foot to another uncomfortably.

"That was in the past," Rebecca announced dryly, "Why are you bringing it up now?"

Abe winced at her words, "I want to say that I'm sorry, Rebecca. I am so, so sorry. I have been so foolish in so many ways."

"I never would have asked you to waste time on me that you should have spent working," Rebecca replied, "I wanted to help you, Abe, not be a burden."

While she kept the same even tone, Abe could detect more hurt than he wanted to imagine.

"Rebecca," he looked up to meet her eyes, "Is there any chance...I still...could you ever love me again?"

It was Rebecca's turn to look down now. She set her jaw and firmly announced, "No, I could not. Now, I need to get back to my work."

As Rebecca marched back to her piles of laundry, she felt as limp as a noodle. She wondered if Abe could tell how completely off-kilter he had thrown her. His words had come as the biggest surprise of her life, and had been too much to process at one time.

"What happened?" Sadie asked, turning away from the laundry that she was placing in a wicker basket.

"He..." Rebecca couldn't go on. She couldn't force herself to speak. She just shook her head and turned back to her work.

Why did Abe have to come back now and mess her life up once again? Try as she might to still them, her emotions were in a blender. She felt like crying and screaming and jumping for joy all at once.

Abe still loved her. Rebecca wanted to chase him down and tell her she was sorry too; she wanted to throw her arms around his neck and tell him that she still loved him.

But she wouldn't do that.

Abe Miller had hurt her once. She wouldn't give him the chance to hurt her again.

Abe couldn't eat his food that night. Instead, he simply sat at his place at the table, picking at the delicious meal that his mother had prepared.

"What's wrong, son?" His mom spoke up as she took another slick of homemade bread, "Are ya just worried about church in the morning? Or is this something else?"

Abe shook his head and knotted his hand into a fist on the table.

"*Ach*, Mom, this is bound to be awful! I tried to take your advice...I tried to follow the Lord and let Him give me strength. I prayed and I did what I thought He wanted, and I just made a mess of things."

Mrs. Miller raised her eyebrows and Abe went on, "I went to see Rebecca Graber today and apologize for the way that things went when we were younger. She had been a good girlfriend to me, and I treated her horrible. I was so certain it was the right thing to do, but now I'm questioning myself entirely. I don't know about following God, *Mamm*, because He seems to get me in some tight places and then leave me completely alone."

Abe fought the desire to cry. Surely, talking to Rebecca had opened up more hurt between the two of them than it had fixed. Now, the idea of seeing her in the morning made the idea of preaching a sermon even worse.

"Following the Lord doesn't mean that you always get your way or that life is always easy," Mrs. Miller finally spoke up, "But at least you know you're doing what's right. You don't have to understand why God's asking you to do these things...it's just your job to trust and obey. If you felt like God was leading you to go make things right with Rebecca, then you did the right thing. I don't know how tomorrow's going to turn out for you, Son, but I know God's going to be by your side. And, if you follow Him and it's a disaster, we'll just have to accept that as His will."

Abe couldn't argue with her logic, although he wasn't sure that he liked it. Instead, he just looked down at his plate and mentally started thinking of other communities they could move to if things went too bad.

Chapter Six

It was Sunday morning; the day that Rebecca Graber had been dreading all week. As the Amish community slowly filed into Amos Harshbarger's house for the twice-a-month church service, Rebecca felt like she was going to be sick.

As if having Abe preach wasn't bad enough, talking to him the day before had made things that much worse. Rebecca felt so nervous and unsure of herself, she didn't know if she could stand to remain seated for the entire event. Fearing she might bolt when she saw him, Rebecca sat down beside her sister, hoping Sadie would hold her down if she tried to escape.

Abe had never been more nervous than he was while one of the other men led the congregation of Amish through the regular hymns and old songs.

He turned toward the sermon notes he held in his hand, looking them over. They seemed so pathetic, so hopeless.

Glancing at his mom, Abe noticed her give him a smile.

Once the singing was over, one of the men announced that it was time to hear from their new minister, Abe Miller. Abe pulled himself to his feet and started toward the front of the room. It felt like his boots were full of lead with each step that he took.

Turning to face the congregation, he took a deep breath. Closing his eyes, he said a quick prayer for courage, and then wadded up his sermon notes and pushed them in the pocket of his black pants.

"I was reading the Bible last night," he announced, completely talking outside of what he had planned, "And I read about David. In the Bible, when we met David, he's nothing but a little shepherd boy."

Abe relaxed as he started talking to the congregation as friends. He explained that David had been nothing more than a little shepherd boy that God had planned to use. On his own, David was no match for the giant Goliath but, when he let God work through him, he was able to put down the mighty man with a small slingshot.

Rebecca felt as if she was glued to her seat. She listened intently as Abe told the story of David and Goliath, and felt as if it was unfolding right before her very eyes. She didn't want to ever leave, she didn't want to move.

"Could David have conquered that giant by himself?" Abe finally asked, "No, he could not. David couldn't do God's work alone, and we can't do God's work alone. We have been promised that we have God to help us accomplish His tasks, but too often we get side tracked by our own abilities and inabilities."

Abe took a deep breath, "Throughout my life, I have struggled with my inabilities. I know the things that I'm good at and I know the things that I struggle to do. When the church board came to my house and told me that I was going to be the new preacher, I could not have been more scared. It caused me to take a deep look at myself and the way that I live my life. For the past twenty-four years, I've been living entirely on my own strength. This job brought me to the realization that I need God in my life. I've made a lot of mistakes in an attempt to only do what I knew I could handle. Now, I see that I'm a very weak man who needs God very much. And I thank each and every one of our community elders for giving me the chance to discover this."

As she listened to him talk, Rebecca felt the years of anger and hurt melt away from her heart. Abe was a changed man, and she could tell it.

Suddenly, she wished that she had never been so harsh to him when he came to apologize. Surely he had sincerely wanted to make things right. But she had said harsh things and hurt him.

All these years, Rebecca had resented the fact that Abe had turned his back on her, and now she had done the same thing to him. He had turned her away because he was afraid, and she had turned him away because she was afraid.

She had to make things right.

Abe breathed a sigh of relief as he sank back down in his seat on the hard wooden bench. The church service was now over and the community was starting to file out to the yard where they would have a picnic in the warm spring sunshine.

"Thank you for getting me through that, God," Abe breathed a sigh of relief.

People continued to come to his side, praising him on the sermon and stating that they'd never heard a better message.

Surprisingly enough, Abe discovered that he had actually enjoyed delivering the morning message. He found himself looking forward to the next service and was anxious to get home to study for another sermon.

"Are ya coming out to eat?" Mrs. Miller asked as she walked past her son.

Abe nodded slowly, "Go on out, *Mamm*, I'll be there in a minute."

When Abe thought the house was empty, he leaned his head against the back of the wooden pew and closed his eyes.

"Excuse me," a soft voice spoke near his ear.

Sitting up suddenly, Abe realized that Rebecca Graber had come to stand beside him.

"I need to talk to you, Abe," she said in little more than a whisper. Cautiously, she sat down beside him, and took a deep breath.

"I am so sorry for the way that I treated you yesterday," she began, "I didn't mean to be so harsh. I was simply afraid."

"Afraid of what?" Abe managed to ask, turning to look her in the face.

Rebecca looked down at her hands which were folded in her lap, "I was afraid because I know you could break my heart if you wanted," she said gently.

"Then...you do still care?" Abe dared to ask, almost afraid of her answer.

Rebecca looked up at him, her blue eyes filling with tears, "Ever so much, Abe. Ever so much. I don't think I have ever loved you more."

"And I love you, too." Abe exclaimed. Reaching out, he put his hand on hers.

"I know we're too old for the young peoples' meetings," Rebecca finally whispered, "But would ya want to come to my house for supper tonight?"

Abe nodded his head, his heart filling with joy.

Despite the fact that he had felt like God abandoned him the day he went to see Rebecca, the Lord had been with him all along and had been working out the wrinkles in Abe's life. He knew that, now, he and Rebecca would finally have the chance for a truly good relationship together: a relationship that was no longer based on fear, but instead on their mutual trust in and reliance on God.

AN AMISH AUTUMN

ABBY BARKER

"And eventually I'll take over my father's business. I made an entire dining room set the other day and only one of the chairs wobbles when you sit on it."

Olivia took a long sip of her tea to keep from having to comment on another boring man's boring story. Her parents watched her expectantly from the other side of the table. This was the third "date" they'd set her up on this month and she wasn't having any of it. It wasn't exactly fair that she wrote him off before he even walked through her parents' front door, but she couldn't help it. It was exhausting to force smiles when these men showered her with cliché compliments, or fake a laugh when they cracked a bad joke about this season's crop yield. Over and over again she sat in front of these men, and over and over again she quickly turned them down when they asked to see her again.

Her parents had her best interests at heart; there was no doubt about that. An unmarried twenty-one-year-old Amish woman was basically considered an old maid. They couldn't bear the side-eyed glances and whispers she got when they went into town, but Olivia couldn't care less. She wasn't interested in marriage, and this her parents knew, but she also had slowly lost interest in the Amish religion itself. That fact she kept from them. She didn't know if their old fashioned hearts could take it.

Despite her protests, Olivia continued to sit, ankles crossed and tea in hand, at her parents' kitchen table with nice-young-Amish-boy after nice-young-Amish boy. The only thing that made these meetings barely sufferable was imagining what each man would look like if they were some kind of animal. This man – Was his name Caleb? – had a head of spiky brown hair and a pointy nose. Olivia imagined him as a giant hedgehog snuffling the air as he droned on about some aspect of carpentry that she couldn't begin to care about. The thought of his tiny little paws holding a hammer made her smile, which timed perfectly with Caleb's fifth compliment of the hour.

"Your hair reminds me of a nice, polished red oak, which is harder to work with than you might think."

"I've got to go! Excuse me. Lovely to meet you, Kevin."

Olivia jumped up out of her chair, waved awkwardly goodbye, and bolted out the door. She knew she'd have to explain herself to her parents later, but she just couldn't take it anymore. Every person they insisted she meet was exactly the same. What made them think she'd connect with one Amish carpenter more than another? It didn't matter what she said to them, they'd always respond the same way: "Olivia, a good Amish woman marries a good Amish man. Don't you want to be a good Amish woman?"

No. She didn't, actually, but up until this moment she didn't know how to tell them. If she had to sit through one more afternoon tea with a man who wouldn't know excitement if it hit him in the face she thought she might explode. Olivia had been casually planning her escape from the small town where she grew up for some time now, but it hadn't really been serious. Leaving the Amish world was a serious decision, one that she probably couldn't take back. She had a childhood friend who left for rumspringa and never came back who she still exchanged letters with. Abigail always said she could come live with her for a while if things ever got to be too much. That offer was looking better by the second.

After pacing around her neighborhood for almost an hour, Olivia returned home. Mama prepared dinner in the kitchen while Papa read the Bible at the table. Neither looked up at her when she entered.

"Mama, Papa, I need to talk to you."

"Oh, now you want to talk. Why couldn't Chatty Kathy have paid us a visit while we tried to explain to Caleb why our ill-mannered daughter ran out the door without a word? Hmm?" Mama chastised as she walked around the room, slamming dishes.

"Mama's right, Olivia, you do owe us an explanation but you shouldn't have behaved that way in the first place. We raised you better than that."

"Yes! You *raised* me. Past tense. You treat me like a child that you're trying to marry off! I'm through with this constant parade of men that I'm not interested in, and never will be. You know what? I wanted to do this a different way but it doesn't seem to be an option. I'm through with being Amish too! I'm going to stay with Abigail in Philadelphia until I figure out where I want to go. I'm sorry, but this isn't the life for me."

Olivia's parents were stunned silent. Mama even stopped clanging the dishes. Olivia wasn't sure if they were going to react with fury or sadness until her father finally spoke.

"That's unfortunate to hear. I think it's best if you pack up your things and leave as soon as possible then. Your mother and I wouldn't want to force you to stay a minute longer."

Mama started chopping carrots, but didn't say a word. This was it, then. Olivia was officially leaving. She felt a small pang of regret, but couldn't see how she could take it back now. Papa went back to reading the Bible and it was as if she had never been there in the first place. Olivia shamefully went to her room, packed up her things, and started walking into town. Her parents didn't even say "goodbye."

Her escape fantasies never included logistics so finding a ride to Philadelphia wouldn't be easy. She didn't have much money or know anything about the bus system. She didn't even know which direction to head in. Olivia decided to walk into town and hope someone there might be on their way to the city. She had been walking along the road, grumbling to herself for sometime when a man and his daughter pulled up next to her in their buggy.

"You're looking a little lost. Can I offer you a ride?"

"I'm not lost. I know exactly where I am, thank you very much. I'm on my way to Philadelphia."

"Pardon my intrusion miss, but Philadelphia is in the other direction."

Olivia felt her face turn red.

"I knew that. I was just...taking a detour."

The man smiled knowingly.

"I tell you what. How about you come back with me so I can drop my daughter off at home and then I'll drive you to Philadelphia."

"I don't know..."

"It's a lovely night for walking, but even so you're still quite a ways away. Amy here will make you a cup of tea while I tend to the horses and then we'll be on our way, hm?"

Olivia didn't make a habit of getting into buggies with strange men, but the offer was too tempting to refuse. Besides, the man had a daughter. It wasn't like she'd be going home alone with him. Embarrassed, she relented. The man hopped out of the buggy to help her stow her bag and then assisted into the seat next to his. Amy leaned forward from the backseat to talk Olivia's ear off.

"Hi! My name's Amy and I'm eight years old. I have a doll and her name is Maggie, but I don't know how old she is. You're pretty, just like Maggie. I'm glad you're coming to my house 'cause then you'll get to meet her and see what I mean. Your hair is just like hers. Why were you walking in the road all by yourself? Doesn't your daddy have a horse and buggy that he can drive you around in? How far away is Philadelphia? I know it's in Pennsylvania because my teacher told me."

"That's enough, Amy. Please don't scare our guest off before she even gets to our home."

Amy giggled and sat back in her seat but not before whispering.

"Pardon me for not introducing myself sooner, my name's Andy. Amy's already introduced herself. And who might you be?"

"Olivia. Olivia Fisher. I live, or lived, a few miles up the street from here."

"Lived?"

"My parents thought it best that I leave."

Andy could hear that Olivia was reluctant to give up any more information than that and he didn't push her.

"Well, alright Olivia formerly from up the road, let's get you a cup of tea and then back on your way to Philadelphia."

"I make tea really good," Amy piped up. "Daddy just started letting me heat up the kettle on my own and I'm getting really good at it. I only forgot about the water one time! Daddy doesn't have a wife to make him tea so I have to do it for him."

"Okay, Amy. Olivia doesn't need to hear our whole life story right away. At least get her that that cup of tea first."

Olivia hid a smile. She wasn't used to people being so willing to talk about themselves. Her family excelled at leaving things unsaid and sweeping feelings under the rug. When they did finally bring themselves to talk about things it almost always ended with some sort of blowout, which is exactly why she found herself in a buggy with an unmarried father and his daughter. Olivia wondered what happened to the girl's mother, but even as forthcoming as they seemed she knew that topic would most likely be off limits.

The unlikely trio carried on down the road for a ways before they reached a neighboring town.

"That's our house!" Amy yelled, pointing at a small, but colorful home at the end of the street. The house was painted a cozy yellow with small red flowers painted around the bottom. It was definitely the most vibrant building on the street, only matched by the stables, which were painted sky blue and covered in clouds. It was nothing like the modest, identical homes that filled her neighborhood.

"Wow, it's beautiful! I didn't know anyone could have a home like that."

"We got some backlash from the neighbors at first, but it eventually grew on them."

"Can I ask why did you paint it that way?"

"Mama thought it was boring the way it was! She said, 'I want the outside of my house to feel just like the inside: happy and full of life!'"

"Your mama sounds like a lovely person."

"Oh, she was. She's in heaven now, but Daddy says we have to keep the house the way it is so Mama can look down and find us."

Olivia felt a pang in her chest. This happy and outgoing little girl didn't have a mother. It didn't seem fair. She looked over at Andy who continued to steer the buggy into the stable without taking his eyes of the ground in front of them. She could see from his expression that hearing his daughter talk about her dead mother pained him. It definitely wasn't fair, Olivia decided. This exceptionally kind little family shouldn't have had to face such a tragedy.

"I'm so sorry, Amy. It's a very nice way to remember your mother."

"It's okay. It doesn't make me sad anymore. I know she's happy as long as we're happy."

Olivia looked back to see Amy flash a bright smile before she jumped out of the buggy and bounded into the house. Andy exited the vehicle as well before walking to Olivia's side to offer her a hand.

"I'm sorry about that. You didn't sign up to hear a couple of stranger's family history today. Amy can be a chatterbox sometimes, whether it's appropriate or not."

"Oh, please don't apologize! I'm just sad to hear that a sweet girl like Amy had to go through something as tragic as losing her mother. Not to mention what you want through."

"Yes, well, she's an amazingly resilient little person as it turns out. She's my whole world now. As long as I have her I can make it through another day. Do you have any children?"

Olivia didn't know exactly how to respond immediately. Andy took this to mean he crossed a line and began apologizing.

"You know, I shouldn't have asked that. I'm sorry. That's your business and no one else's. I don't know what I was thinking."

"No! It's not that. I just...no, I don't have any kids. I don't know what I want yet. That's sort of how I ended up here, I guess."

"You don't owe me an explanation. Let's go inside and drink that tea I promised. Amy will have already put the kettle on by now. She's very enthusiastic about her new skill, if you haven't already noticed."

They both laughed and their tension melted. Olivia realized she had only known this man for about an hour but she already felt so comfortable with him. She wondered if he felt the same about her.

The inside of the house not only matched the outside in spirit, but also in decoration. Fresh flowers littered the kitchen and living room, placed artfully next to a variety of colorfully upholstered furniture. But the focal point of the whole home had to be the huge mural that covered an entire living room wall. From floor to ceiling the scene depicted a sprawling meadow dotted with trees, flowers, and herds of content horses. The image was painted with such careful detail that Olivia could see distinct personalities reflected in each of the horses' eyes. Even after seeing the outside of the home, this mural was so beautifully painted Olivia couldn't help but let out a gasp. Amy noticed her reaction from her place in the kitchen.

"Do you like it? Mama did that one too! Some of those horses are the ones in our barn. Mama would take them out to that field and let them run free for a while, but they always came back to her. I think they liked her just as much as she liked them."

"Your mother was an incredible artist, Amy. Do you paint too?"

"I did. Do you see that little tree next to the big tree?"

Olivia's eyes followed Amy's outstretched finger to a spot right near the edge of the mural. A pair of trees stood side-by-side, one a bit taller than the other. When she looked more closely she noticed that the two trees looked almost human. The taller one was womanly, while the shorter looked to be a small child. Amy's mother had subtly painted them as trees, a detail that would go unnoticed by anyone who wasn't looking for it. She felt tears well up in her eyes. She could feel a mother's love just by looking at the painting.

"I helped paint the leaves on the smaller tree because that's me! And the bigger tree is Mama. Mama didn't paint Daddy as a tree because she said, 'Daddy isn't like a tree. He's like the sun that watches over us and helps us grow.' But now I think Mama's more like the sun because she's up in the sky looking down on us now."

Olivia didn't know what she could say to the girl without bursting into tears so she only smiled. She heard a whistle come from the kitchen.

"The water's ready! Come sit with me and have some tea."

Andy had gone back out to the barn to prepare the horses and buggy for their ride to Philadelphia so it was only Amy and Olivia at the table. It had been a while since Olivia had been one on one with a child. She babysat when she was practically a child herself, but she hadn't done that for sometime now. Luckily, Amy wasn't one to shy away from a conversation and had plenty of things she wanted to talk about.

"Do you still live with your mama and daddy?"

"Kind of. I did. But we all decided I shouldn't live there anymore."

"Is that why you were walking in the road?"

"Yes. I was trying to get to Philadelphia to meet my friend. I was hoping I could live with her."

"You can live with us if you want! We have a spare bedroom and everything. I'll even let you play with Maggie if you get lonely. She's good at that."

"Thanks, Amy. That's very sweet of you, but you should probably talk to your daddy before inviting strangers to move in with you."

"You're not a stranger. You're Olivia! Besides, he wouldn't mind. He likes you, I can tell."

Olivia blushed without meaning to. She hoped that Amy wouldn't notice. She was young, but probably precocious enough to call her out on it if she saw. At that moment Andy walked back into the house, a frustrated expression on his face.

"It doesn't look like I'll be able to give you that ride after all, Olivia. At least not today."

"Oh no! What happened?"

"I took a look at the buggy and it appears I've busted a wheel. It's a miracle we even got home on it, the thing's ready to fall right off. I'm sorry, Olivia. I can't go into town to buy a new wheel until the shop opens back up tomorrow, and even then I'm going to have to give the old buggy a complete examination to make sure nothing else is about to go before I'll feel comfortable driving all the way to Philadelphia and back. Now, you're welcome to stay with us – I promised you a ride to the city and I plan to follow through when I get this all figured out – but if you don't feel comfortable with that I can see if one of the neighbors can give you a ride back to your parents house."

Olivia thought over her options. Showing back up on her parents' doorstep was out of the question. She'd have to give them a false apology and start right up going on blind dates again, an idea that she couldn't stomach. She was again surprised at how comfortable she was with the prospect of staying in this family's home over night. They had jut met that evening, but she knew she could trust them and she could tell by Andy's tone and Amy's face that she wouldn't be putting them out. It seemed like an easy decision to make.

"I would be happy to stay the night. Thank you so much for your hospitality. You've done more for me in just a couple of hours than most have done their whole lives."

"It's no trouble at all, really, and I know Amy likes the company."

Amy nodded vigorously in agreement.

"Please let me cook dinner tonight to show you my thanks."

"Oh! Yes! I'll help!"

Amy jumped up from the table and grabbed Olivia by the wrist.

"Let me show you the garden. We can pick some vegetables to cook for dinner!"

Andy gestured at them to head outside and Amy ran off, trusting that Olivia would follow. Olivia turned to Andy on her way out the door.

"Thanks again for this. I don't know what I'd do if I had to go home tonight. Things there, they aren't great. Your kindness means everything to me."

"You have a good heart, I can tell. I know you'd do the same for us if the tables were turned. As long as you're here, this is your home too. I don't want you to worry about it anymore than if you were under your own roof. And I mean your own, not your parents.'"

He touched her reassuringly on the shoulder and she felt a shiver go up her spine. His kindness overwhelmed her on its own, but up close she noticed how his smile complimented his bright blue his eyes. The loss of his wife aged his features but from this distance his true age shined through. He couldn't be much older than she was. To be twenty-something years old and a widower with a daughter, Olivia couldn't imagine. She started to feel something more than just grateful. She ran out the door before her trademark blush could betray her feelings.

In the garden, Amy had already turned her skirt into a makeshift basket and was filling it with an assortment of fresh vegetables. Looking at the varied spread, Olivia was unsure what meal the enthusiastic little chef had in mind, but she had spent her fair share of time in the kitchen and was up for the challenge.

"What have you got there, Amy?"

"Veggies!" she yelled, a tomato rolling out of her skirt.

"And what is it that you wanted to make for dinner?"

"Veggies!"

Olivia couldn't help but smile at the head of brunette curls bobbing up and down through the garden scooping up far more vegetables than they'd need to feed a group of three. She'd always been convinced that children weren't in her future, but seeing how much she enjoyed being around this bright and helpful little girl almost made her reconsider. Cooking dinner with the child of a man who saved you from being homeless for a night was different than being a mother, but Olivia at least got a taste of what it might be like.

Amy ran over to her holding a curved zucchini across her face like a big green smile.

"Look! The zucchini is happy to be our dinner!"

Olivia grabbed a carrot from Amy's collection and held it up to her own mouth.

"The carrot is too! I think they want to be tossed together in a stew. That way they can relax in a nice hot tub before they join us for dinner."

Amy burst out laughing and dropped the edge of her skirt scattering all of her vegetables in the dirt. This only made her laugh harder and caused Olivia to join in. The two girls were laughing hysterically, surrounded by a sea of dirty vegetables when Andy walked out of the house to see what the commotion was about. He stood silently for a moment, relishing in his daughters laughter before speaking up.

"Who's going to cook dinner if my two chefs are doubled over in the yard?"

"We will, Daddy! But we're not chefs anymore, we work at a veggie spa!"

"A veggie spa?"

"It's where all the veggies go to relax before dinner. It was Olivia's idea!"

"Is this true? Are you opening a veggie spa in my home?"

"Only temporarily. Amy and I decided to make a stew but thought it would make the veggies more comfortable if we referred to the pot as a hot tub instead. They'll be more delicious if they're relaxed!"

Andy joined in on the laughter as the three of them picked the vegetables up off the ground and brought them inside. Andy set the table while Olivia chopped the veggies and Amy tossed them into the pot. They prepared supper in a comfortable silence until Amy started to giggle and talked to the simmering veggies.

"I hope you're having a good time in there because when you're all cooked and squishy I'm going to put you in belly and there's no spa in there!"

Once the veggies were all cooked and squishy, Olivia filled three bowls with the steaming stew and set them on the table. They all took their seats, linked hands, and Andy said grace. Olivia wasn't used to a spoken grace. At home her family silently prayed before each meal, but this was special.

"Dear Clair, thank you for looking after us and making sure we always have enough to feed ourselves, and the occasional guest," he smiled at Olivia. "We're blessed to share this meal with our new friend, Olivia. I can't help but think you had a hand in putting her in our path today."

It was then that they dipped their heads for a more traditional silent prayer. Olivia said a quick grace to herself before letting her mind drift back to the first grace. Clair must be Amy's mom. She'd never heard anyone say grace to a dead loved one before, but it made sense to her. Clair certainly was looking after her family from heaven. Of course they'd want to thank her, and if she did have a hand in bringing her together with them Olivia wanted to thank her too.

The meal progressed normally, filled with small talk and quiet laughter, until the conversation turned to Olivia's parents.

"Is your Mama in heaven too? Is that why don't live with her anymore?"

"No, my Mama's not in heaven. She just...we're not getting along right now. There are some things that we don't agree on so I can't go home."

"Oh, I'm sure if you both just said you were sorry and hugged she'd forgive you. She's your mama and she loves you. I bet she wishes you were home right now."

"That's good advice, but I wish it was that simple," Olivia responded, fighting back tears.

"You don't have to answer if you don't want, but can I ask what it is that you disagree with them about?"

If this were any other Amish family she wouldn't have dared sharing her doubts about being Amish, but she knew they'd hear her out. Olivia took a deep breath and felt a jolt of confidence after looking into Andy's kind eyes.

"My parents can't see me as a complete person until I'm married. They've been setting me up on dates since I was sixteen just to try to expedite that process. I'm not even sure I want to get married, and definitely not to any of the men they bring home. They say I'm practically an old maid in our community and I don't know if I even want to be a part of a community that thinks that way. I told them all of this and then they asked me to leave. I have a friend in Philadelphia who offered me a place to stay if anything like this ever happened."

"Olivia, I'm so sorry you have to go through this," Andy looked as if he had something more to say but glanced wearily at Amy. "Sweetheart, why don't you run off to get ready for bed?"

"Okay. I can't wait until I'm old enough to stay awake for grownup talks."

Amy hugged her father goodnight and did the same to Olivia, adding on an extra squeeze.

"You could marry a rock for all I care. I'm glad Mama introduced us today. Goodnight, Olivia."

Once Amy had given them one last wave from down the hall and closed her bedroom door for the night, Andy finished his thought.

"When Clair died my neighbors came around with all sorts of casseroles, loaves of bread, and condolences. They all basically said the same thing: 'We're sorry for your loss. Take as much time as you need to mourn. Clair was a lovely woman.' They were all well meaning, but it only took a couple of weeks for them to start asking when I would find a 'new mother' for Amy. Can you believe that? A 'new mother.' I was furious. No one would be able to replace Clair in Amy's heart, or mine. The fact that they thought I could just go out and pick up a new wife, like going to the market, was awful and absolutely none of their business. They made me seem like a bad father and a bad man for not conforming to their idea of a 'Perfect Amish Family.' I was so angry with them for twisting all the beautiful parts of being Amish into something negative. It took a long time and a lot of doubt about being Amish for me to realize that. It wasn't being Amish that caused than to be this way, it was being inconsiderate."

Olivia considered this. Could she remain Amish and still have the life she wanted? Just because her parents had one vision of a "good Amish girl" didn't mean that was the only one, or the right one. There was no way that the man sitting in front of her could be considered anything other than good, even if he didn't conform to his neighbor's ideals. She thought she knew what she wanted, but now she wasn't so sure.

"Anyway, you didn't ask for a monologue from me. Let me show you where the guest room is."

The room had a small bed in one corner and a dusty easel and pile of art supplies in another. An unfinished portrait of Amy as a toddler sat on the easel. Her toothy smile filled the center of the canvas and her face was partially encircled by a ring of wildflowers. It looked like the artist was only a few flowers away from finishing.

"This was Clair's studio. We turned it into a guest room when she passed, but I couldn't bear to get rid of her things and it felt too sad to hang an unfinished painting so I just left everything be. We keep the door shut but Amy comes in here sometimes to feel close to her mother.

She knows that painting's of her, but she tells me that when she looks at it she sees Clair."

"It's a shame she didn't get the chance to finish it. It's such a lively portrait of Amy."

"It is. Amy's always been that way. I worried after her mother died she'd lose that joy for life but she held on to it. Don't get me wrong, it's never easy for a young girl to lose her mother but she's been stronger than I could have ever imagined."

"She's an amazing little girl. I'm glad to have met her."

"I know she feels the same about you. I know we've only known you for half a day, but it feels like so much longer. I'm happy to have met you too Miss Olivia Fisher. Sleep tight."

Andy's blue eyes and sincere smile would be the last thing Olivia thought about before she fell asleep that night.

In the morning, Olivia awoke to the sounds and smells of frying coming from the kitchen. Amy stood on a stool whisking eggs in a bowl while her father scrambled them in a pan. Three place settings sat on the table and a kettle of water had already been boiled, presumably thanks to Amy. She slept a little longer than she intended, surprisingly comfortable for spending the night in a strange bed. When Amy noticed Olivia standing in the doorway she jumped down off her stool and rushed to give her a hug.

"Good morning, Olivia! I hope you slept okay. I was almost too excited to sleep because we get to spend the whole day together while Daddy goes into town!"

"Only if you don't mind keeping an eye on her while I run a few errands. I have to see about getting this wheel fixed so we can get you to where you're going."

Olivia felt a twinge of sadness thinking about leaving so soon, but she only smiled and patted Amy gently on the head.

"Of course I'll keep an eye on her! It's no trouble at all; especially after all you two have done for me. We'll have a great time!"

After breakfast, Andy assured them he'd be back as soon as he could and started to walk into town. The moment he his horse stepped foot into the road Amy started rattling off a list of things she and Olivia could do together that day.

"Since Daddy didn't take all the horses we could ride them down to the river and have a picnic, or we can go raspberry picking behind Mr. Miller's barn – he doesn't like it very much but as long as we don't get caught – or we can go climb the pile of fallen logs in the woods, or sneak into Mr. Miller's hayloft and drop stones in front of the horses to scare them. Don't worry, I'd never drop stones *on* them. That would be mean."

"I think maybe we should leave Mr. Miller's property alone. I don't want to get in trouble with your father."

"Let's take a picnic out to the river then! We have some bread and cheese I can pack into a basket and then we can go swimming!"

Amy quickly went about gathering everything necessary for a picnic by the river while Olivia got the horses ready for the ride. When they arrived at the river Amy wasted no time jumping in. She had led them to a particularly calm section complete with a swinging rope tied to a tree. Olivia watched happily from the bank as Amy jumped in and out of the water for hours.

When they finally arrived back at the home some time in the evening, Andy was already there fixing up dinner. Olivia noticed a new wheel propped up against the barn. The wheel wouldn't find its way onto the buggy for a few more weeks. Andy always had an excuse as to why he didn't have time to put it on, while Olivia constantly made up chores she had to finish "tomorrow." It quickly became clear that everyone in that house didn't want Olivia to ever make it to Philadelphia.

One early morning, Andy disappeared into the barn and didn't emerge until the afternoon. The wheel disappeared with him. When he finally emerged ran immediately to where Olivia was tending the garden and explained the situation.

"Wheel's fixed, but it's going to take a little more time than I thought to fix up our old buggy."

"How much more time?"

"Hard to say. I have to have some custom pieces made and then I have to put them on the thing. Maybe a couple weeks? Maybe a month? Maybe I'll just keep breaking pieces off to keep you from leaving."

Andy grabbed Olivia's hands and looked into her eyes.

"I know it's only been a couple of weeks, but they've been the happiest weeks I've had in a long time and I know Amy feels the same way. I'm not asking you to replace anything we've lost; I would be a fool to do that. All I'm asking is for you to be yourself here with Amy and me. I know this wasn't what you set out to find when you started walking that day I picked you up, but I think it's something special. Being a part of a loving family shouldn't take away your freedom, it should make you feel even freer. I want to give you that, but only if you want it. I love you, Olivia."

Olivia had to grip Andy's hands hard to keep from falling over. He was right. This wasn't what she was looking for, but it seems that it was looking for her. She realized that it was the men her parents set in front of her that she was opposed to, not marriage. The idea of marrying the kind, sincere, amazing man in front of her – and being the stepmother to his equally incredible daughter – brought her more joy than the thought of Philadelphia ever could.

"Of course. Of course I'll stay! I love you, too, Andy. You and Amy. I can't imagine being anywhere else."

Andy wrapped her up in his arms and kissed her tenderly on the lips. She never thought she could feel this much passion and affection for any man, but here he was literally sweeping her off her feet. She'd even found a man that would make her parents happy and for the first time in weeks she looked forward to seeing them again.

Amy soon realized what was going on and buried herself in Olivia's skirt. This was a completely different kind of love that she vowed to cherish for the rest of her life. At dinner that night she said her own quiet prayer to Clair, who she was sure was responsible for this entire situation. Olivia thanked her and promised to always treasure the unexpected gift she'd been given. Holding hands around the supper table with her new little family, Olivia felt freer than ever before.

LOST AND FOUND

STEPHANIE SWIFT

Rebecca Thompson put on her sunglasses and silently counted the steps it would take to reach the waiting limo from where she stood in the hotel lobby.

One...two...three...four...

Fifteen. Just fifteen steps and she would be in the safe confines of the backseat, away from the paparazzi peeking from behind the bushes near the entrance, ready to pounce on her as soon as she stepped outside.

Taking a deep breath, Rebecca secured her purse on her shoulder, pushed open the swinging door, and walked hurriedly to the waiting limo. Sam, her chauffeur, jumped from the vehicle as soon as he saw her approaching and hustled to the rear passenger door to open it for her. Unfortunately, in just a matter of seconds, the paparazzi had already swooped in.

"Miss Thompson! Miss Thompson! What can you tell TV Daily about your reprisal role in Lucky Girl?" one reporter asked.

"I'm sorry, Trudy, but you know I can't discuss the details of that right now. If you'll excuse me..." she responded.

Camera's flashed from every direction and Rebecca was momentarily blinded as she pushed her way through the ever-growing crowd.

Just seven more steps.

The reporters were always annoying but today they seemed positively relentless. She was used to a few of the regulars haunting her every step, but this was ridiculous. One particularly bold reporter attempted to stop her by grabbing her arm, but she jerked away from him and continued walking.

"Rebecca! Rebecca! Miss Thompson! What is your response to the rumor that your boyfriend has reconciled with his ex-wife?"

Rebecca stopped in her tracks and turned to face the reporter who asked the question. She laughed. Surely, he couldn't be serious. Her boyfriend, Colton, would never do such a thing. First of all, he despised his ex-wife. Secondly, he knew Rebecca would choke the life out of him if he even considered it.

"Where did you hear that?" she asked.

The others huddled around her with their microphones, cell phones, and various other recording devices. She lowered her shades and stared at the reporter who questioned her. His expression jumped back and forth between excitement over getting her attention and trepidation over what he may have just gotten himself into.

"*Where* did you hear that?" she repeated.

The young man put the microphone to his mouth.

"We received a tip from a credible source who saw your boyfriend and his ex-wife kissing in a corner booth at Shapiro's Restaurant last night. What is your response?"

Rebecca sucked in a breath. Unfortunately, she couldn't refute the statement because she honestly didn't know where Colton had been the previous night. After rehearsing scenes with some other Lucky Girl cast members on set, she had come home late and crashed.

Rebecca thought for a moment. Did she even speak to Colton yesterday?

No, this couldn't be true. It had to be another fabricated lie, like the numerous others she'd been subjected to during her acting career. Rebecca pushed the reporters out of her way and continued walking toward the waiting limo. There was only one way to find out for sure.

Sam opened the car door and Rebecca slipped inside and scooted to the opposite side of the limo, away from the glaring camera flashes and nosey journalists. Sam managed to fight his way through the throng of people, and when he took his place behind the steering wheel, Rebecca wasted no time in deciding her route.

"Take me to Colton's house."

* * * *

Rebecca bolted from the limo as soon as Sam brought it to a stop in front of Colton's mansion, not even bothering to wait for him to open the door for her. She paused for a moment and glanced around the property, noticing right away that Colton's new Jaguar and his antique Chevy Chevelle were parked inside the garage, which usually indicated he was home. Whether he was alone or not was a different matter altogether.

"Sam, please take the limo back to the hotel. This may take a while."

He looked apprehensively from Rebecca to Colton's house and back again.

"Are you sure, Miss Thompson? I don't mind waiting."

As much as she appreciated his concern, right now she had just one goal in mind.

"Please, Sam. I'll be fine. I'll call you when I get ready to leave."

He gave her a wistful look before getting back in the limo and making his way down the long and winding driveway. When he drove around a bend and out of sight, Rebecca approached the front door and pounded on it several times with her fist. For a moment, all was quiet. Then the door opened, but instead of his butler, it was Colton himself on the other side.

"Rebecca! W-what are you doing here? I thought you were supposed to be on set today," he stammered.

Rebecca glanced past him and into the enormous adjoining den, which appeared to be empty. She stepped forward and looked at him more closely. Upper lip twitching. Shifty eyes. Perspiration on his brow. Rebecca pushed him aside and walked in the house.

"Where is she?" she asked.

Colton tried to utter a reply, but it was so obvious he was lying. She knew him better than he knew himself, and he was one of the worst liar's she'd ever seen. Rebecca headed for the stairway leading to the second floor, but before she could take the first step, Colton jumped in front of her and blocked her path.

"What are you doing?"

She darted around him and raced up the stairs, taking them two at a time.

"I think I'm the one who should be asking YOU that question!" she yelled.

He caught up to her rather quickly, and each time he tried to stop her, she would push him out of the way. He switched between shouting obscenities to begging her to "be reasonable", which only added to her growing suspicion. When Rebecca arrived at Colton's bedroom, she yanked open the door before he had the chance to stop her.

She expected to find his ex-wife, Julia, lying in his bed, but she was nowhere to be seen. Rebecca quickly scanned the room, but it was empty. Colton stood nearby, panting from exertion, with his hands on his hips and never once meeting her gaze.

Something wasn't right.

Rebecca looked around the room again, and that's when she saw it – a tiny speck of blue peeking from underneath a pillow on the floor beside the bed. She walked over and kicked the pillow out of the way, unearthing a lacy blue bra lying beneath it. Her heart started racing and she could feel each pulse as it throbbed in her veins and made her head ache. Colton never said a word.

"Come out, Julia! I know you're here!" she screamed.

It was silent for a long time, but then Rebecca heard the closet door being opened slowly. The tension in the room was so thick you could cut it with a knife, and she didn't have to guess who was there. She knew. She felt the anger steadily building inside of her before she glanced toward the closet and saw Julia standing there, with nothing but a thin bed sheet covering her body.

She wanted to yell – to scream – to rip her hair out – and Colton's too. But what could he say that would make it all just a bad dream? This was really happening, and there was no way he would be able to discount something that was so blatantly obvious.

Rebecca left the room before she burst into tears. They could break her heart into a million tiny pieces, but she would die before she let them see her cry. Colton followed her as she ran for the stairway, and when he made the mistake of grabbing her from behind, she whirled around and slapped his left cheek...*hard*. The sound of it echoed through the empty corridor, and he clutched the bannister to keep from falling as he stumbled backward.

Rebecca continued down the stairway and went straight for the front door, grabbing a set of keys from atop a table in the foyer on her way out. There was no way she was going to wait for Sam or stoop to calling a taxi company, and she knew from her many times driving it that the keys belonged to Colton's Chevelle.

"Rebecca! What are you doing? STOP!"

She had to get out of there before she snapped. The air felt thick and burned her lungs as she ran toward the garage, with Colton not far behind. Rebecca jumped in the Chevelle and locked the doors. Seconds later, he was banging on the driver side window.

"Get out of my car, Rebecca!"

She glared at him as she put the keys in the ignition and roared the engine to life.

"I bought it for you, Colton, so technically it's MINE! Now move out of my way!"

She put the car in reverse and slammed on the accelerator, but unfortunately Colton jumped back before she had the chance to run over his toes. When she put the car in drive and started down the driveway, he tried to run after her, and as she watched his lone figure grow smaller and smaller in the rear-view mirror, Rebecca finally let the tears fall where they may.

* * * *

The New York city limit sign had long come and gone before Rebecca realized she'd left her purse in the limousine. The need to get as far away as possible had been too great to focus on anything else, and now as she coasted on fumes down an abandoned Pennsylvania dirt road, the severity of her situation was hard to ignore.

She knew she should have gone straight to her hotel, but she also knew that in no time at all Colton would show up, and she just couldn't face him again. So, she headed west, away from New York and the heartache and humiliation. She didn't have a cell phone, a paper map, or a GPS. She simply turned the wheels toward the open highway and never looked back.

When the fuel ran out and the engine began to sputter, Rebecca pulled over beside the road and stopped. *Now what?* The last gas station she'd passed had been several miles back – not that it mattered. She had no cash, no credit card, and the only change she could find inside the car was a measly 49 cents.

Rebecca leaned her head against the steering wheel. She didn't want to go back, but she'd spent the past five years with Colton, and she had no clue how to move forward either. The news had probably broken to all the major TV stations by now, and there would be no way to hide from it. All she really wanted was to disappear for a while.

She looked at the barren land surrounding her and she had to laugh when the realization hit her that she was off to a very good start. There was no way anyone would be able to find her in such a deserted area. The thought thrilled her but terrified her at the same time.

Rebecca got out of the car and leaned against the door. It was early afternoon, and there wasn't a vehicle or house as far as the eye could see. The hot August sun was unforgiving as she wiped the tiny beads of sweat from her brow and started walking. She didn't know where she was or how far she had to go to find help, but she did know she couldn't just sit inside a sweltering car and do nothing.

As Rebecca walked and walked for what felt like an eternity, she hummed her favorite songs, recited her Lucky Girl lines, and did whatever else she could think of to keep her mind occupied and not focus on the way her feet and back ached with every step. After rounding a curve, she spotted in the distance what resembled a horse pulling a buggy with two people sitting inside. Her heart began to pound with a mixture of hope and fear. What if they passed her by? What if they were serial killers?

She laughed. *Stop it, Rebecca. The heat is making you delirious.* As they got closer, she saw an elderly man at the reins and a woman sitting on the seat beside him who appeared to be about the same age. Both were dressed in Amish attire, and Rebecca expelled a sigh of relief. She moved over to the edge of the road and hoped they would stop and offer some assistance. When the man pulled up on the reins and brought the horse and buggy to a halt in front of her, she wondered briefly if they might recognize her from her acting roles. Did she want them to or not? Honestly, she couldn't decide.

"*Guder nammidaag!*"

Rebecca raised a brow. She had no idea what he said, but his smile was so big and warm, she immediately felt at ease.

"Hello," she replied. "Could you please tell me where I am? I'm afraid I might be lost."

They exchanged glances before the woman leaned forward to look at her more closely. Her brown eyes pierced right through her, leading Rebecca to take a cautious step backward.

"You're in Lancaster, Pennsylvania," she said. "Where are you from?"

Okay, so they didn't recognize her.

Rebecca tossed around her options. She could tell them, but then again that might lead to her returning to New York sooner than she wanted to. On the other hand, she could lie, but lying to an Amish person felt very sacrilegious and would possibly warrant a one-way ticket to Hell. As she struggled with the imaginary devil on her left shoulder and the angel on her right shoulder, the man and woman whispered to each other and continued with the worried glances.

"Dear, are you alright? You seem...disoriented," the woman said. "What is your name?"

Disoriented. That was it! She could pretend she'd lost her memory! If anything, it would help her bide her time until she could decide what she wanted to do, and since this was acting...well, it wouldn't *really* be lying.

"I...I don't know."

More glances.

"Do you have family here?" the man asked.

Rebecca thought about Colton to try and make herself cry, but that only made her angry, so instead she did what always worked when she needed to cry on demand – she thought about her first puppy, a sweet little Poodle named Amber, who died when she was fifteen years old. Within seconds, the tears were swelling in the corners of her eyes.

"I'm not sure," she replied. "I'm so sorry. I'll stop troubling you now."

She turned to walk away, but the woman scrambled down from the buggy to stop her. When she grasped her elbow, Rebecca turned to look at her with tears rolling down her cheeks. It had the effect she wanted, as the woman placed her hand over her heart and gave Rebecca the most pitiful look.

"*Neh*, dear. You're not troubling us at all. We would like to help you, if we can. My name is Hannah King, and this is my husband, Eli."

He tipped his hat to her, and she smiled at them both as she wiped the tears from her cheeks with the hem of her shirt sleeve.

"We live in a small community not far from here. We were just returning from Lancaster. It's getting late, but we can take you there tomorrow. Perhaps the sheriff will be able to help you."

Their willingness to aid a stranger took her by surprise. Being from New York, she wasn't used to such hospitality, and it filled her with guilt. Maybe this wasn't such a great idea.

"Thank you, but you don't have to do that. I'll walk to Lancaster..."

She tried to leave, but Hannah stopped her again.

"You will do no such thing. We have a spare bedroom, and you could probably use a hot meal and some rest."

She simply wouldn't be swayed, so there was no turning back. Hannah climbed up on the buggy and sat down beside Eli and then motioned for Rebecca to sit next to her. When they were situated, Eli made a strange whistling sound with his mouth and the horse went into an easy gallop.

She feared the ride to their home might be awkward and quiet, but she couldn't have been more wrong because Hannah talked nonstop. Rebecca learned their only child, Hope, had moved to a different Amish community in northern Pennsylvania with her husband and their four daughters. Hannah earned money making quilts and selling them in one of the Amish storefronts in Lancaster, and Eli worked as a blacksmith.

When they arrived at their home, Rebecca felt as if she'd learned their whole history, which made her feel even more uncomfortable, given the circumstances. They asked her questions, probably hoping to stir up a memory or two, but she played her part and acted aloof until they eventually stopped with the inquiry.

"Ah, Daniel! There you are!" Eli remarked. "Let's get these horses some extra grain before you leave. They've had a busy day, especially this one."

Rebecca leaned forward to see who he was talking to and she spotted a man approaching them from the opposite side. He took the reins from Eli before helping him and Hannah step down from the buggy. Unsure of what to do, Rebecca stayed put.

"Daniel, this is...well, it's a long story, but she's our guest and will be staying with us tonight."

He was very handsome and they appeared to be about the same age. He had on Amish attire, much like Eli was wearing. He was quite tall, with tanned skin and short brown hair. His face was cleanly shaven though, unlike Eli, who had a long gray beard.

"*Gut'n owed*. It's nice meeting you."

There it was again – more of that strange language she didn't understand. Daniel held up a hand to help her down, and when she placed her hand in his she noticed right away how warm his skin was, which sent an unexpected chill up her spine. Despite her wobbly knees, she managed to plant her feet firmly on the ground without stumbling over them and making a fool out of herself. While Daniel led the horse and buggy toward the barn on the far end of the property, she did her best not to stare after him.

"Now, let's get you settled in for the night," Miss Hannah said.

She smiled. Perhaps this wasn't such a bad plan after all.

* * * *

The sun was just starting to rise in the east as Daniel jumped from his wagon and walked hurriedly toward the King's front door. He was operating on little sleep, but he'd started out at first light so he could get there early and talk to their houseguest. Mr. Eli had shared very few details with him the night before, other than finding her walking the main road alone and that she appeared to have some type of amnesia. Even so, he had to admit he was very intrigued by this stranger who was, without a doubt, NOT from their community. When Miss Hannah opened the door, he did his best not to appear too enthusiastic.

"*Guder mariye*, Daniel. Come in."

He stepped inside the den and removed his hat before following her to the kitchen. Since he began working as Mr. Eli's assistant two years prior, he'd become accustomed to their usual morning ritual, which included eating breakfast with the couple before work commenced. Daniel's happy mood diminished when he walked in the kitchen and discovered Mr. Eli was the only other person in the room.

"*Guder mariye*," he announced.

The elderly gentleman nodded as Daniel took his place at the table, and he smiled at him, trying his best not to appear as downtrodden as he felt. When Miss Hannah put four heaping plates of scrambled eggs and bacon on the table, he felt his spirits lift again. She was still here! He grinned a bit more widely than he probably should have, and when the beautiful stranger entered the kitchen just moments later, he accidentally dropped his fork, causing it to clang loudly against the metal plate.

She was busy fiddling with the buttons on one of her sleeves, but when she looked up and saw him sitting there, she smiled.

"*Guder mariye*," Miss Hannah said. "I hope you slept well."

She gave Miss Hannah a curious look before sitting down on the opposite side of the table from him.

"*Guder mariye* means good morning," Daniel explained.

That seemed to help because she nodded as if she understood.

"I did sleep well. Thank you," she replied. "Miss Hannah, did you wash my clothes for me while I slept?"

She ran her fingers over the silky material of her shirt and gave Miss Hannah another strange look, as if the thought of her doing so surprised her for some reason.

"*Yah*, I did. They were quite dusty from your walk yesterday, so I washed them for you."

When she looked his way, Daniel noticed her eyes glistened with unshed tears. She cleared her throat and tried to inconspicuously wipe the teardrops from her eyes, but Daniel caught it, even if no one else did.

"That was so nice of you, Miss Hannah. Thank you."

When the couple reached out to join hands with them and pray over the meal, he wished he was sitting next to her so he could hold her hand. She glanced nervously at them before they prayed, but she gave them all a tentative smile before placing her hands in Miss Hannah and Mr. Eli's and bowing her head.

After Mr. Eli prayed, they talked about the day's work ahead of them while their guest sat quietly by and listened. He tried not to stare at her, but she was so beautiful it was difficult not to. Her raven-colored hair hung in waves that barely touched her shoulders, and her eyes were such a pale shade of blue they appeared almost gray. She seemed quite shy, which fascinated him even more. Who was this stranger and where did she come from? He wanted and needed to know.

When Miss Hannah mentioned taking her to Lancaster to speak to the sheriff, he saw an opportunity and took it.

"Miss Hannah, I can do that for you. Mr. Talbot said Mr. Eli's parcel should arrive in today's mail, so I can stop by the post office and check on that while I'm there. I mean, if it's okay with the two of you, of course."

He probably jumped at the chance a bit too abruptly, by the way the couple smiled at each other when he mentioned it. His glanced across the table as the heat began to rise to his cheeks, but thankfully their guest didn't object to his offer. After a brief discussion, Mr. Eli agreed to let him accompany her to Lancaster, and Daniel nodded, not trusting himself to speak for fear of embarrassing himself even further.

When they were finished with breakfast, she followed Daniel out the front door to his wagon. He planned to help her climb up the step, but she was much quicker than he was, and she was already seated and ready to go before he even had time to adjust his hat. After he took his place beside her, he couldn't help but notice how close she was.

Their legs were almost touching, and even though he knew creating some space between them would be the gentlemanly thing to do, he just couldn't bring himself to move over. As he guided the horse and wagon toward the road and away from the King home, she glanced his way and smiled.

"Thank you for doing this," she said.

He looked forward, not trusting himself to stare at her for too long in case he accidentally veered them away from the road and into a ditch.

"You're welcome."

The clothes she wore reminded him of the plain women in Lancaster, who often wore pants and brightly colored blouses. The shirt she had on was made from a soft material he'd never seen before, and the color brought out the blue in her eyes. The wind picked up just then, and a few tendrils of her hair brushed against his cheek, making him inhale sharply as his heart thumped erratically.

"I noticed there's no electricity and no televisions or phones at the King's house."

He smiled. No, she certainly wasn't Amish.

"We don't believe in modern technology the way plain people do. It has a way of distracting us from living the way God intended."

She gave him a quizzical look.

"Plain people?"

He had to admit her innocence was quite endearing.

"People who aren't from the Amish faith and community."

She nodded, but she also grew quiet, which made him wonder if he'd said something wrong.

"Have you been able to recall any details from your life?" he asked.

She glanced sideways at him and shrugged her shoulders.

"No, not really. What about you? Do you live here? Are you married?"

Her sudden barrage of questions surprised him, and at first, he didn't know how to answer. She seemed curious, but he couldn't tell if her curiosity was genuine or if she was just trying to be nice.

"*Yah*, I live here, and I'm not married. I've worked as Mr. Eli's assistant for the past couple of years. He wants to retire from the blacksmithing trade soon, and he doesn't have a son or grandson to pass it on to, so he's training me to take over his business."

She became quiet again as she glanced around them at the rolling hillside, and he didn't interrupt her train of thought. He couldn't imagine being locked inside her mind, with no recollection of where she came from or even what her name might be. It had to be a very lonely and frightening thing to endure.

"I think it's nice. Your way of life, I mean," she said. "It's so peaceful here. I slept better last night than I have in a very long time."

Her comment confused him, since she supposedly couldn't remember anything about her life, but he didn't say anything. When they reached the end of the road and turned left onto the main road to Lancaster, she sat up straight and folded her hands in her lap. She wore a few pieces of jewelry, but there was no wedding band on her left hand, unlike some of the plain women he knew in Lancaster.

"I'm guessing you aren't married..."

Before he could finish his sentence, she turned abruptly in her seat to face him. He didn't look at her, but he could feel her eyes boring a hole straight through him.

"Why do you say that?" she asked.

He pulled back gently on the reins to make his horse stop walking. Her demeanor had completely changed, and he saw the way her eyes shimmered with tears. He felt like kicking himself, even though he had no clue what he'd done.

"I apologize. I didn't mean to pry. I just noticed you weren't wearing a ring on your left hand. I have plain friends who are married, and they all wear a gold band on this finger."

He touched the finger beside her pinkie on her left hand, and she looked at it longingly before a tear escaped and started rolling down her cheek. Before he had the chance to talk himself out of it, he gently wiped it away with his hand – a move that seemed to surprise her just as much as it did him.

"I'm so sorry. I never meant to make you cry."

Her eyes widened and she turned back around and looked straight ahead. She didn't say anything for a long time, and Daniel took that as a sign to leave her alone. He flicked the reins and the horse galloped forward, but he didn't say another word. Perhaps it was best to just let it go.

"I never stopped to consider it, but I suppose you're right," she said. "There isn't someone special in my life."

She said it so softly it was almost a whisper. He wanted to disagree with her and reiterate the fact that he didn't think she was *married* and not that she wasn't seeing someone, but he remained silent instead of risking tripping over his own tongue.

Neither of them spoke again throughout the rest of the trip, and when they arrived at the post office in Lancaster, he jumped down from the wagon and walked around to the other side to help her down, not that he expected her to accept his help. He did it simply because he'd been taught it was the right thing to do.

She surprised him by placing her hands on his shoulders, and he had no other choice but to grab her waist. She didn't let go right away when he set her down on the ground, and they stood so close he could feel her breath on his skin, but her expression was a difficult one to read. He did notice the way her beautiful blue eyes no longer sparkled the way they had earlier as they sat around the King's kitchen table, and that alone made him sad.

"I can come with you to talk to the sheriff, if you like."

She dropped her hands and stepped away from him. He pointed to the sheriff's office, which was four doors down from the post office, but she shook her head.

"No, thank you. I need to do this by myself."

He nodded.

"I'll meet you back here. Just take your time. No rush."

She smiled at him, but she didn't make a move, so he started for the post office to give her some space. Right before he stepped inside the building, he caught sight of her walking toward the sheriff's office. He knew he should feel happy over the possibility of her discovering where she belonged, but he also knew once that happened she would more than likely disappear from his life...and that dose of reality hurt a lot more than he expected it would.

* * * *

Rebecca sat on the edge of the bed and contemplated her next move. After tossing and turning most of the night, she removed the long flannel nightgown Miss Hannah gave her and put on her clothes. She could tell they'd been washed again, which made her feel even more guilty, if that was possible.

She couldn't get Daniel off her mind. He was so kind and such a gentleman, and there was no sense in denying it...she was falling for him. No, she wouldn't continue with this charade. She couldn't. Leaving him, however, was another heartache altogether.

She'd managed to sidetrack the sheriff's office as soon as she saw Daniel disappear into the post office, but it wasn't easy. The residents of Lancaster were particularly curious over her, and she couldn't move an inch without someone watching her every move. She worried that someone might recognize her, but no one approached her. (A fact that filled her with relief but also irritated her. Did these people NOT watch TV at all?)

Rebecca returned to the wagon seconds before Daniel did, and she concocted another story by telling him the sheriff promised to check the missing person's database frequently and stay in contact with her. He didn't question it, but she thought for certain she was busted when they passed a man on the way home who was hauling the Chevelle with a tow truck. Daniel turned and stared at it when they passed by, but if he noticed the New York license plate, he didn't mention it.

Rebecca hung her head in shame. This wasn't acting. She was deceiving good, honest people – simple as that. She picked up her shoes and tip-toed to the bedroom door, trying to step as lightly as she could to keep the wooden floor from creaking beneath her. They had no electricity, so thankfully there was no alarm system to alert the King's she was leaving. Once outside the house, she slipped on her shoes and took off in the direction of the main road that would lead her back to Lancaster.

She had no idea what time it was, but the sun was starting to rise. Before she could reach the main road, she caught sight of Daniel approaching in his wagon. She frantically searched for a place to hide, but there were no trees, no dwellings...just acres upon acres of open farmland in every direction. She moved to the side of the road as he drew near, but when he stopped in front of her, she couldn't bear to look at him. She knew without a shadow of a doubt that one look would give her away, and she just couldn't bring herself to hurt another person, especially not Daniel.

"You're leaving?"

His deep voice broke through the stillness and made her tremble. Rebecca turned away from him and walked faster toward the main road. She heard the wagon creak and then Daniel's feet hit the ground, but she refused to slow down.

"Wait!" he called.

No, she couldn't do this. She wanted revenge over Colton, but not like this. It wasn't worth it.

Daniel caught up to her and grabbed her arms from behind to make her stop. She thought he would let go right away once he had her still, but he didn't, and the heat from his hands seared through the thin material of her shirt and made her tremble once again.

"Please don't go," he whispered.

Rebecca closed her eyes and fought back tears. His breath was hot against the back of her neck, and she caught herself leaning into him, enjoying the warmth.

"I can't do this anymore. I've been lying to you, Daniel...to all of you. I never lost my memory. I was running away."

He dropped his hands and moved away from her. When she turned around to confront him, the look on his face was all it took to make the tears fall. His expression was a mixture of shock, sadness, and disbelief.

"My name is Rebecca Thompson, and I live in New York. I'm...I'm an actress."

He opened his mouth, but no words came out.

"I'm so sorry, Daniel," she continued, before he tried to stop her. "I discovered my boyfriend, Colton, was cheating on me, and I just took off. That car...the one you saw yesterday on our ride home...it was mine. I ran out of gas, and I didn't have any money, so I got out and walked. That's when the King's found me."

He removed his hat and ran his fingers through his hair as he paced back and forth. She waited for him to say something, but he was silent for so long she feared he never would.

"But why? Why would you lie? Why didn't you just tell Miss Hannah and Mr. Eli the truth from the start so they could help you get home?"

She wiped the tears from her face and crossed her arms over her chest.

"At first I wanted to disappear, but then I met you, and that changed things. I didn't want to leave."

He stopped pacing and looked at her. She closed the distance between them, and when he tried to back away, she grabbed his arms to keep him from doing so.

"We come from two very different worlds, Rebecca..."

She nodded solemnly before looking down and shuffling her feet in the dirt. She didn't know what to say, and she certainly couldn't argue with him. After all, he was right.

Before she could decide how to respond, he was pulling her close and claiming her mouth with his own. It all happened so suddenly, but it was a welcome surprise, and he didn't release her until she was left breathless and weak in his arms. Rebecca held on to him tightly to keep from falling.

"Does this mean you want me to stay?" she asked.

He took a step back, and when she saw the sadness in his eyes, she immediately wished she could take back the question.

"I'm afraid it's not that easy," he replied. "There are customs our people have been abiding by for many years..."

Rebecca nodded and held up a hand to keep him from saying anything further.

"It's okay, Daniel. I understand."

He gently brushed his fingertips against her cheek and smiled.

"I didn't say it was impossible."

Rebecca's spirits soared. Perhaps there was hope for them after all. Still, she was afraid to move, to breathe...to break the spell that might make it all come crashing down around her.

"You've got to tell the truth, Rebecca. We can't try and build something together based on a lie. It won't work."

She nodded.

"I know, and you're right."

He glanced toward the sun that was now peeking over the horizon. She wondered for a moment if Miss Hannah and Mr. Eli were awake, and if they had noticed she was gone or that Daniel was late for work.

Her heart ached for so many different reasons – partly from guilt, but most of all from wanting something so badly that might never happen.

"What about New York, your career...and your boyfriend?"

She sighed.

"The only thing left for me in New York is my job, and I'm not even sure I want that anymore. I do know that I'm through with Colton. That should have ended a long time ago."

Rebecca placed a hand against his chest before standing on her tiptoes so she could kiss him again. Her heart raced when he pulled her into his embrace instead of pushing her away, like she feared he would. It felt wonderful, but most importantly, it felt *right*.

"Daniel, I don't have all the answers. This is new to me too, but I promise you I want this to work, and I'm ready to do whatever it takes to make that happen."

Her answer seemed to satisfy him, and he smiled as he grabbed her hand and began pulling her toward the wagon.

"Okay, then the first thing you need to do is tell Miss Hannah and Mr. Eli the truth. They are the closest thing I have to a family, and I know they will do whatever they can to help us."

Rebecca groaned as he helped her into the wagon. It wouldn't be easy, but as she watched Daniel sprint around the wagon and take his place on the seat beside her – grinning the whole time – she knew without a doubt that it would be worth it in the end.

"We'll get through this...together," he said.

Rebecca huddled close to his body and smiled.

Together – what a beautiful place to start.

AMISH DEPARTURE

DEIDRA SCOTT

Chapter One

Lizzy Swartz closed her eyes and took in a deep breath of the spring air. The scent of cut grass and freshly plowed dirt put a smile on her face. She lifted her face upward, allowing the sun to warm her skin.

There was nothing like a spring day spent working out in the garden. Just the time in God's outdoors put a song in Lizzy's heart.

Suddenly, something hard hit her in the arm. Lizzy opened her eyes to see her fifteen-year-old brother, Abe, preparing to launch another clod of dirt in her direction.

"*Ach*, Abe!" Lizzy exclaimed, "Will ya never start to grow up?"

Abe stood up straighter and gave his dirt ball a toss across the garden, "Probably not," he replied, a boyish grin spreading across his handsome face.

Lizzy couldn't help but smile back, "Well, don't just stand there – pick up a garden hoe and get to work!"

"Yes, ma'am!" Abe returned in a silly tone and anxiously grabbed one of the tools, "I wouldn't want you to decide to whack me *gut* with one."

"Where's Grandpa?" Lizzy asked as she set to work chopping out some of the weeds that were starting to grow between the rows.

"He ran out to the mailbox," Abe replied.

They worked in silence for a few minutes until Abe finally asked, "Lizzy, what do you think would have happened to us if Grandpa hadn't taken us in?"

Abe's question made Lizzy stop for a moment. My, but hadn't she asked herself that question at least a dozen times? It had been almost twelve years since their parents had been killed in a tragic buggy wreck. The Amish community had been hit by hard times already with a rough drought that killed most of the area crops and left everyone feeling the strain financially. No one had enough money to take on two extra Amish children. At one point, there had been talk of sending Lizzy and Abe to foster care...but then Grandpa had stepped in.

A widower who was already shouldering the heavy job of being bishop to the Amish community, Grandpa had taken them in as if they were his own children. Although they called him Grandpa, he was completely unrelated to Lizzy and Abe.

"I don't know, Abe," Lizzy finally said with a deep sigh, "But I certainly thank God every day for sending him our way."

Abe slowly nodded his head, "*Jah*, me too."

They both worked in silence.

Grandpa had not provided them with a fancy life full of impressive possessions, but he had done his part to give them a stable home that was rich in love. Over the years, he had worked hard to instill steady morals, a love for their Creator, and a respect for hard work in the hearts of both Lizzy and her brother.

"Have you got any plans for tonight?" Abe finally asked.

Lizzy felt her face go red with embarrassment. "*Ach*, Abe," she exclaimed, "Aren't you a nosey one! Maybe I do and maybe I don't!"

"I already know you're going out with Matt Christner!" Abe exclaimed, tossing another clod of dirt at his sister, "I saw him in town and he told me."

"Well, isn't he the big mouth!" Lizzy returned with a laugh.

While Lizzy and Matt had been friends for most of their lives, they had only recently started dating. Although their relationship was new, Lizzy had already recognized that Matt was the man she wanted to eventually marry.

Lizzy's thoughts were cut short when she heard Grandpa whistling as he walked up behind her.

"Mail's here!" He announced cheerfully as he handed Lizzy a letter from her cousin in Pennsylvania.

"Didn't I get anything?" Abe asked.

"You can open mine," Grandpa told him with a laugh, tossing a handful of envelopes in his direction, "Let me know if I got anything other than bills. I'm going out to the calf barn to check on some of the babies."

Abe flipped the mail around in his hand, sorting through it for anything exciting. Stopping at one envelope, he gave a shrug and tore it open.

"Oh, Abe," Lizzy let out a laugh as she started to read the letter from her cousin, "Sally says..."

"Wait, Lizzy!" Abe exclaimed, cutting her short. Before she could protest, he called out, "Grandpa, come back here! It's important!"

Grandpa turned and hurried back to Abe's side, anxious to see what was wrong.

"*Ach*, what's happened now?" He asked, reaching for the letter.

"It nothing bad, Grandpa!" Abe exclaimed, "Its good news! Your uncle who died left you a lot of money! A lot! Yee-haw!"

"Well, I'll be," Grandpa whispered as he scanned over the document, "It surely does look like I've inherited quite a sum of money...from an uncle I don't even remember."

As Grandpa read the letter once more, Abe gave his hat a toss in the air and grabbed his sister by the shoulders, "Lizzy...we're rich!"

Chapter Two

Until Grandpa had a chance to go see the lawyer in town, they all three agreed not to tell a soul about the letter or the possibility of the inheritance. While Abe was convinced that they truly were now wealthy, neither Lizzy nor Grandpa shared his confidence.

That night, Lizzy's boyfriend Matt arrived at their house on his buggy. Although it was hard to think of anything other than the inheritance, getting to go somewhere with Matt seemed like it might distract her from the thought of money.

As she rode along beside Matt on his buggy, Lizzy found that the idea of getting her mind on something else was entirely too far-fetched to be possible.

Suddenly, Lizzy realized that Matt had hardly spoken a word to her since he picked her up at her house.

"*Ach*, Matt," she muttered, suddenly feeling ashamed of herself, "Here we've been riding together for miles and I've hardly spoken a word this whole trip. I'm sorry. I'd better watch it or you'll be picking you out a new sweetheart!"

Turning to look at Matt, she realized that he wasn't laughing or even smiling at her comments. Instead, it seemed like a dark cloud was over his handsome face.

"You shouldn't be apologizing, Lizzy," Matt replied with a deep sigh as he turned the reigns over in his hands, "I should be the one doing that. I'm not much company tonight. Probably not the best day to be takin' ya out to eat, but I sure hated to cancel. Wouldn't want you to pick out a new beau either."

Studying her boyfriend's sad face made Lizzy feel like crying herself. She knew that her Matt had been going through a rough year. His mom had been diagnosed with cancer and, although the treatments seemed to be working, Lizzy realized the family was still dealing with a lot of stress and uncertainty.

Reaching out to pat him on the shoulder, Lizzy found herself searching for the right words to say but coming up short.

"Matt," she finally said with a sigh, "The Lord hasn't forgotten about your family – he has a plan."

Matt slowly nodded his head, but Lizzy wondered if his faith was getting shaky.

The next morning, Grandpa got up early to hitch up the buggy and drive into town to see a lawyer. Although Grandpa warned Lizzy and Abe that the letter was probably nothing more than just a fake, it was impossible not to notice the hopeful glimmer in his eyes.

Waiting for Grandpa to get home was about enough to drive Lizzy mad. The hours seemed to pass so slowly and, every time Lizzy glanced toward the driveway, her heart sank as she realized Grandpa was no where in sight.

Trying to make the time pass faster, Lizzy busied herself with chores around the house. By afternoon, Lizzy had already scrubbed all of the hardwood floors, hosed off the porch, and washed the windows.

"Still no sign of Grandpa?" Abe asked as he stepped into the kitchen, looking for an afternoon snack.

Lizzy shook her head as she lowered one of the windows, "I hope he's okay."

The barking of their dog sent both Lizzy and Abe to the front door.

"He's home!" Abe squealed, jumping like a little kid as he pushed past Lizzy and started out toward the barn where Grandpa was unhitching the horses.

Not wanting to be left out, Lizzy followed close behind her brother.

By the time they reached the barn, both Lizzy and Abe were out of breath.

"Grandpa," Abe gasped, grabbing his side with his hand, "Grandpa, what happened? What did he say?"

"Help me unhitch the horses, Abe," Grandpa replied solemnly as his leathery hands set to work taking the bits out of the animals' mouths.

Abe stepped up and started working alongside his grandfather, his mouth still going much faster than his fingers, "But Grandpa, what happened in town?"

"*Ach*, Abe, we'll talk once we're all inside."

"But we're all out here, Grandpa!"

Despite Abe's pleading, Grandpa remained firm. Watching him lead the horses to an empty stall where he poured them some fresh oats, Lizzy felt her heart sink. There was no way the letter could have been true.

Once they were finished, Grandpa sat down at the kitchen table while Lizzy hurried to set a plate of fresh cookies and a glass of milk in front of him.

"Sit down, Lizzy. Sit down, Abe." Grandpa instructed.

Abe practically jumped into his seat and Lizzy felt like she couldn't grab the chair fast enough.

"Children," Grandpa finally said with a laugh, "I don't know how to tell you this...but the letter was real and the money is now in the bank. We truly are rich!"

Chapter Three

While Grandpa wouldn't say just how much money he had inherited, Lizzy realized that it must be a lot.

Sitting around the table that night, Grandpa explained that the money was something they needed to use for good purposes.

"I know how easy it is to simply waste money," Grandpa told them as he finished off Lizzy's delicious meal of homemade sweet rolls, applesauce, fried potatoes, and pork chops, "And I don't want us to waste what we have now. Before we start spending a lot of it, I want you two to come up with some ways that we could use the money to do something *gut*...not just for ourselves, but for the entire community."

Abe lowered his head, obviously a bit disappointed at the thought of having to share with the rest of the Amish.

"Can we buy a few things for ourselves?" Abe asked with 'humph'.

"Of course," Grandpa opened up his wallet and began sorting through his bills, "I know that there are things around the house that we need. Lizzy," he motioned for her to hold out her hand, "This is for you and Abe to spend on the things that we need."

Unfolding the bills that Grandpa had placed in her hand, Lizzy gasped as she whispered, "*Ach*, Grandpa, this is one-thousand dollars!"

Grandpa nodded slowly, "I think it's time that we made some improvements around here. Let me know if you need more than that."

Staring at the money, Lizzy wondered how on earth she could ever begin to think of spending one-thousand dollars on anything.

The next morning, Lizzy discovered that spending money was much easier than she had expected. When she had her driver take her to the grocery store, she planned to only spend within her usual budget. For the last five years, Grandpa had given Lizzy the sole responsibility of shopping for their weekly groceries with a very small amount of money. Lizzy had learned how to be resourceful by making purchases in bulk, off-brand items, and using coupons.

As she entered the store that Thursday morning, it seemed harder than ever to stick to her budget. Just knowing that she had one-thousand dollars to use as she saw fit made shopping seem like an entirely different experience.

When she left the grocery, Lizzy had a cart load full of groceries she would never normally purchase. After seeing how high the bils was, Lizzy promised herself she would start using their money more wisely.

Despite Lizzy's resolution to be more careful with the money, it seemed less possible with each day that passed.

Grandpa and Abe were astonished with her expensive meals that included thick steaks, but enjoyed them so much that she wasn't scolded; in fact, Grandpa reminded her to keep buying what they needed because the money was unlimited.

Although Lizzy had always enjoyed baking, the convenience of running to the store to pick up ready-to-eat loaves of bread, pies, and cookies was almost more than she could stand.

When wash day came, Lizzy even hired a driver to take her to the local laundry mat where she was able to get them cleaned and dried in a fraction of the time it took her to do the job by hand at home.

As soon as Lizzy realized that some of their clothing needed to be patched, she chose to toss the damaged items in the trash rather than keep them. When she went to pick out new fabric, the thought of sewing sounded so time consuming, that she simply hired one of the local Amish seamstresses to do the work for her.

While her work load dwindled, Lizzy took the opportunity to enjoy time reading books and going on walks in the fields.

Lizzy wasn't the only one who enjoyed the chance to indulge in some expensive luxuries. Grandpa decided that, rather than clean out the barn by hand, he would hire someone with a bobcat to do it for him.

"We need to make some serious barn repairs, too." Grandpa told Abe and Lizzy, "I'm thinking we could just hire a team of the Amish carpenters to come fix it up for us." Pausing for a moment to think, he added, "Honestly, might be even more sensible to just build a new barn all together."

"Grandpa," Luke started slowly, "I'll be sixteen next month and the age to go to the young peoples' gatherings. Do ya suppose you could just buy me a new buggy to drive? The old one's so worn out and it sure sends me in the air when I hit a bump – I'd hate to find me a pretty girl and send her sailing off the buggy seat!"

They all laughed and Grandpa nodded, "*Jah*, I don't see how a new buggy could hurt!"

Within a few days, the entire family wondered how they had ever lived on such a tight budget in the past.

Chapter Four

Saturday night, Lizzy and Matt went out on a date to the local *Englisher* restaurant in town. Whenever they went out to eat, it was a treat, but today seemed somewhat less of a thrill. With all the money that Lizzy had been spending on fancy food to cook at home, the meal seemed rather boring.

Once they had finished eating, the waitress came by and asked, "Do you want to order some desert?"

Looking at Lizzy with a smile, Matt announced, "I guess we'll take a piece of chocolate cake with ice-cream. We're splitting it, so we'll need an extra plate."

"*Ach*, Matt, sharing is such a bother." Lizzy couldn't hide her disgust at the thought of being frugal, "Let's get one for each of us!"

"Lizzy," Matt reached out and put his hand over hers, his tone little more than a whisper, "I don't have the money..."

"Don't worry about paying for it, Matt," Lizzy announced, digging through her black purse for some money, "I'll be covering the bill tonight."

Looking up at the waitress, Matt said, "Just give us one. If we need more, I'll buy a second."

The waitress looked uncomfortably from Matt to Lizzy and then back to Matt. Taking a deep breath, she nodded her head, "I'll put in the order for one. Just flag me down if you decide to get two."

As soon as she had left them alone, Lizzy found herself rolling her eyes, "Come on, Matt! What's the matter? I said I have the money. Why can't you let me pay for it myself?"

Matt shook his head slowly, "Lizzy, you don't understand. I don't want to have a girlfriend that pays for her own food. I like saving back my money and bringing you out to eat."

Unwilling to cause a scene or risk totally running their time together, Lizzy gave a curt nod and ended the conversation.

When the waitress delivered their cake, they ate in silence. Lizzy simply could not understand why her boyfriend was so stubborn!

"I'm sorry we fought in the restaurant," Matt whispered when they had finished eat and were seated side-by-side on his buggy, "I don't want us to ever argue about anything. Will ya forgive me...and still let me bring you to the young peoples' meeting Sunday night?"

Lizzy couldn't help but smile. Staying mad at her boyfriend wasn't worth the effort. Sliding over closer to him, she took a deep breath, "I'm sorry, too. *Ach*, Matt, I never would have brought up paying for it if I knew it was going to make you upset." Leaning her head against his shoulder, she took a deep breath of the night air and wished that there was some way that he, too, could enjoy the money her family had been given.

The next morning, Lizzy, Grandpa, and Abe went to church at Joe Eicher's house. Like all Amish people, the community met every other week at one of the homes of an Amish family. Preparing for the church service was a huge event that generally involved hours of cleaning and set-up.

On the way to the Eicher's house, Lizzy noticed Grandpa eyeing various things along the road. When they went past the Amish schoolhouse, he slowed the buggy down to a crawl as he pointed out the sagging roof and needed repairs.

During they church service, Lizzy watched Grandpa stare absent-mindedly at his hands. As bishop of their Amish community, Grandpa was not in charge of preaching but rather helped the entire group stay true to their beliefs.

Once they had sung the last song and church was ready to end, Grandpa stood up and raise a hand in the air.

"Before we go out to eat this delicious meal, I have an announcement to make," Grandpa said.

At his words, women stopped gathering their children and everyone returned to their seats to listen quietly to what their leader had to say.

"As everyone here knows, I've never been a rich man," Grandpa announced, "So you can imagine my surprise this past week when I discovered that I have inherited a large sum of money."

Lizzy listened as the Amish began to whisper and buzz with excitement.

"Driving past the school house today, I noticed that it needs some serious repairs." Reaching into his billfold, Grandpa pulled out a check, "That's why I want to call Teacher Simon forward to receive a check for twenty-thousand dollars to make the necessary repairs."

Everyone gasped and then began to clap their hands.

"*Wunderbargut*!" Someone yelled out in excitement, "The children won't have to worry about it raining in on their heads any longer!" Everyone laughed.

Giving the congregation a chance to settle down, Grandpa finally announced, "I have something else to bring up, too. I know that this is different, but I want everyone here to take some time to consider this suggestion. My whole life, I've watched the women in our community burdened with the heavy load of hosting church service at their homes. I propose that we step out and build a new church building."

Suddenly, the room went silent.

Build a church? Even to Lizzy, the idea sounded strange and terribly English! Although she saw nothing wrong with the big, impressive churches in the towns, it wasn't their way at all. The Amish were simple folks and holding church within the homes was a tradition that went back hundreds of years.

As the minutes ticked by, there was still no reply to his suggestion. Finally, Joe Eicher stepped up, uncomfortably putting his hands in his pockets and refusing to look at Grandpa, "We'll have a chance to talk about all these things later. For now, my wife invites you outside to have a picnic in our front yard."

Chapter Five

Grandpa didn't stay for the picnic; instead he suggested that they stop at the restaurant in town to buy some food. Lizzy missed the feeling of togetherness she got when she gathered with her friends and family, but certainly wasn't sad to avoid the awkward stares of the others in her community.

That night, Matt pulled his buggy into their driveway at five o'clock. Lizzy had purchased some pre-made hamburger patties in town and had just finished frying them up for her Grandpa and Abe. She would eat at the young peoples' gathering.

"You're making me hungry already," Matt playfully moaned as he leaned over her shoulder. Picking up the box the patties came in, he announced, "*Ach*, we never buy these – too expensive for us poor folks." Although his words were said as a joke, Lizzy noticed something akin to scorn in his voice.

"Who could be here?" Lizzy wondered as she noticed three buggies full of Amish men pull into their drive.

Matt gave a shrug, "Looks like some of the preachers and leaders of the community."

Although she knew it was wrong to spy, Lizzy watched the men hitch their horses to the post by the porch and then step through the front door.

"Hello, Abe," she heard the men greet her brother as they walked through the front door, "Where is your grandpa?"

Lizzy picked up the plate of hamburgers and took them to the table where Grandpa was sitting just as Abe led the group of men into the room.

"Hello there, Mose," the men greeted Grandpa, "Sorry to interrupt your meal."

"No worries," Grandpa returned, "Take chairs. What's on your minds?"

As the men sat down, Lizzy and Matt stepped back into the corner, anxious to see what would happen and hoping not to be sent out of the room.

"*Ach*, Mose," one of the men finally said, "Have you plumb lost your mind?"

"Easy now, Enos," another spoke up, "Mose, we were so thankful for your contribution to the schoolhouse, but I'm afraid that I'm with Enos in asking, what were you thinking when you brought up building a church? You know that isn't the Amish way!"

Grandpa raised an eyebrow, "Come on, men! You know there's no good reason for us not to have a church building."

"Having church within the homes sets us apart from the *Englicher* world," Sam Yoder announced, "If you pull out one of the threads of our beliefs, soon we'll completely unravel! What will keep us from soon having telephones and electricity?"

"And what would be so wrong with that?" Grandpa exclaimed suddenly. In the fifteen years that Lizzy had lived with Grandpa, she had never seen him so upset about anything. She felt almost frightened as she looked into his angry face and watched as it grew redder by the minute.

The other men's eyes grew large as they stared at him.

"Ach," Grandpa finally stormed, "You don't have to like my suggestions at all, but I'll say this...building a church would help our community, and I *am* going to do it! As the bishop of our community, I have the power and with the money, I have the ability."

If the men had looked surprised before, they were totally speechless now. Finally, Enos Bontrager solemnly announced, "I'm sorry you feel this way, Mose. It seems the money has gone to your brain. You maybe the bishop of our community, but that does not mean that you are above reproach. Take some time to consider this idea of yours. If you don't submit to the Amish ways, I'm afraid the community will be forced to go over your head and inflict the *bann*."

The *bann*. Those dreadful words went through Lizzy's mind over and over again. Although she was sitting beside Matt on his buggy, she couldn't pull her thoughts away from that horrible scene at the kitchen table.

Ach, if the Amish chose to *bann* Grandpa, he would be completely forced from their community. He would not longer be able to eat with them – he would be entirely shunned until he repented publicly.

"What's going on with your grandpa, Lizzy?" Matt asked after taking a deep breath, obviously nervous to bring up the uncomfortable subject, "He used to be one of the easiest-going men I ever knew...now he's just acting ornery about everything!"

Lizzy instantly felt her skin bristle. Who was Matt to call her Grandpa names?

"What's that supposed to mean?" She spoke up.

"Come on, Lizzy!" Matt exclaimed, "He's changed...and you have too! Just within a week, it's like you're both different people. I don't like who you're turning into. If things don't change, he's going to end up leaving the Amish entirely."

Lizzy was so furious, it felt like she was on fire.

"Grandpa is one of the best men I know!" She snapped, "If he wants to build a church building, then I'm completely behind him. If you have a problem with it, then maybe we should stop seeing each other. And, if the Amish are going to be so stubborn that they won't accept his gift, then maybe I don't want to be Amish anymore!"

"Lizzy..."

"Just drive," She snapped, folding her arms across her chest and scooting as far away from her boyfriend as she could.

That night, Lizzy sat in her bedroom, thinking about life as she prepared for bed. Lizzy brushed her hair out slowly and stopped to study herself in the mirror. While mirrors weren't usually found in Amish houses, Lizzy had made a secret purchase over the weekend.

Gazing at herself, she tried to gauge how pretty she was compared to the other Amish girls. But wouldn't she be prettier if she had some of that fine paint the *Englishers* wore on their faces!

Instantly, she pushed the thought away, wishing that she hadn't let it run through her mind.

With all that was going on with her grandfather, she truly wondered if they would be left in the Amish church. What Matt had repeated was what all the Amish were thinking. Grandpa was determined to go forward with his plans to build a church...and the Amish community wasn't going to stand for it. There was a good chance that they might get shunned. If that happened, she wondered what Grandpa would do. Would he turn his back on the Amish way entirely? And, if he did, would she go with him?

"Lizzy, Lizzy," she scolded herself, "What are you a thinkin'? Consider Matt!"

But, the more she considered Matt, the more clouded her thinking became. She had been so certain that he was the man she wanted to marry and spend the rest of her life beside, but the money had changed everything.

Lizzy was beginning to like the feeling that money gave her. It made her happy to know that she and her family were a step above the rest of those in their community. She was tired of the work that she had to do as an Amish woman.

If they left the Amish, she would be free to own a washing machine and a drier, a refrigerator, and even a television! Putting aside her brush, Lizzy ran her hand through her hair and took a deep breath.

She was almost scared of what tomorrow might bring.

Chapter Six

All Monday morning, Lizzy found herself looking out the window, afraid that she would see more of the church leaders coming up the drive. In some ways she was frightened, while in others she was almost hopeful.

Grandpa sat at the table, working on a design for the new church. Since the Amish community was set against having it built, he had already contacted a team of English carpenters who could do the work.

That afternoon, someone finally did come up the drive. When Lizzy saw that it was Matt, she couldn't decide if she was more relieved or disgusted.

"Lizzy," Matt took off his straw hat and twisted it between his hands when she invited him inside, "Could we go on a walk and talk?"

Preparing for a lecture, Lizzy braced herself and started across the yard beside him.

Suddenly, Lizzy was surprised when she looked up at Matt and noticed tear drops running down his cheeks. Instantly, her defenses were down and her heart filled with worry for this man she loved so much.

"What's wrong Matt?" Lizzy asked as she reached out to pat her boyfriend on the arm,

"Lizzy," Matt took a deep breath and let it out, "I don't know what to say. My *maam*'s finally going to come home, but now the hospital wants us to start paying our bills. She's got to keep taking treatments and they're expensive, too. Dad doesn't even know how he's going to do it at all. He's talking about selling the farm."

"Selling the farm!" Lizzy exclaimed, "What would you all do then?"

"*Daed*'s talking about moving back to Pennsylvania. There's nothing for us here if we have to sell everything. We can move in with my grandparents until mom's treatments are finished."

"Surely there will be some other way..."

"Lizzy, my dad already took out a gigantic mortgage on the farm. He's not going to be able to pay it back." Shrugging, Matt announced,

"I don't know when we're likely to move, but I'd like the little bit of time we have left together to be good. I'm sorry about last night."

"No, I'm sorry," Lizzy whispered. Reaching out, she wrapped her arms around her boyfriend and pulled him close to her.

That night, Lizzy picked up some food at the restaurant because she didn't feel like cooking. Her heart felt so heavy whenever she thought about Matt and his family. She told Grandpa and Abe. Suddenly, they were no longer concerned about building fancy churches or fighting with the Amish. They just sat together silently, each lost in sorrow over the situation of Matt's family.

"I wish that there was something we could do," Abe muttered softly, "I've always though a lot of Matt's family."

"*Ach*," Grandpa exclaimed as he slammed his hand against the tabletop, "What on earth are we doing? I always looked down on people who had money and were selfish with it...and yet I find that I'm exactly the same way."

"Grandpa!" Abe looked at him in surprise, "How can you say that you're selfish? All you want to do with your money is good! You want to make a better life for us...and you want to help out the church and the community with buildings. How can that be wrong?"

Grandpa shook his head slowly, "In the midst of all our figuring, did we ever stop to even think to ask the Lord what He would want us to do with this money? No. Instead, we chose to plow ahead and do what we thought was best."

Everyone was silent as they looked down at their plates in deep thought.

"Tonight, this ends!" Grandpa announced, reaching out to take Abe's hand in one of his own and Lizzy's in the other, "Tonight we're turning to the Lord to find out what he wants."

The next morning, Grandpa took the money that Lizzy had left over and went to town.

"Well," Abe muttered softly as he worked alongside his sister in the garden, "I sure did enjoy being rich."

"As did I," Lizzy said with a sigh, "But I think I'll be glad to be plain Lizzy once again."

When Grandpa got home, he came out to the garden to work alongside them.

No one said a word until Abe finally ventured to ask, "Do we have anything left at all?"

Grandpa shook his head, "I paid off all of Matt's family's debts and then gave the rest as a donation to the hospital. I've already been to talk to some of the church leaders and apologized for the entire church building idea."

"How are we ever going to make it now?" Abe grumbled, kicking at a clod of dirt with the toe of his work boots.

Grandpa smiled, "I suppose the way we always have...a lot of pinching pennies and patching up clothes. In the end, we did what that Lord wanted and we did what was best for other people who needed the money much worse than us."

"I never did get my buggy," Abe said with a sigh.

"Ahh...that is true." Grandpa gave the teenager a pat on the shoulder, "How about you and I work on that old buggy together. I think if we put some time into it, we can have it good as new."

"And, when you go courting, maybe you can just tell her to hang on tight before you hit a bump in the road!" Lizzy suggested.

They all laughed, finally able to enjoy one another's company without the distraction of money.

Working together silently, they listened to the sound of the birds chirping overhead and enjoyed the cool breeze drifting through the trees.

Prologue

Lizzy smiled to herself as she sat on the homemade wooden swing on the front porch. Although it had been hard to give up the money, she had to admit that a simple life truly was the right one for her.

Looking up from a page in the book she was reading, Lizzy realized that Matt had pulled his buggy into their yard and was coming toward her.

"Hello, Matt," she announced, wishing that she and her beau had never gone through such a rough spot.

Without saying a word, Matt took a seat on the swing beside her.

"It was your grandpa, wasn't it?" Matt asked slowly as he reached out and took Lizzy's hand in his own, "He was the one who helped to cover my *maam*'s doctor bills, right?"

"Matt..." Lizzy looked down at her feet, trying to decide how much she should even start to share, "Ach, Matt, he doesn't want a bunch of people to know. He wanted to keep it a secret. The way Grandpa looks at it, the money wasn't ours to start with...it was just something that God had loaned us so that we could use it to help others. He got off track because of it...we all did, I'm afraid. I'm sorry that I was so harsh to ya, Matt. It was wrong of me. I let the love of money cloud my thinking. Grandpa reminded us that we should pray about what to do with it, and from that point on, it all just became clear."

Matt shook his head, "That's the kind of man I wish that I could be. Lizzy," he took a deep breath, "I'm no where near as great a man as your grandpa, but I'm going to try my best to be a *gut* Amish man who loves his family, helps his neighbors, and serves the Lord. Would you be willing to go through this journey with me...as my wife?"

Lizzy felt her breath catch in her throat and she wondered if she could even start to speak. After all that had happened between them, she was afraid that Matt would be ready to end their relationship completely. She opened her mouth and words wouldn't come out. Instead, all that would come were tears of joy.

"Oh no," Matt teased jokingly, "Looks like you're not very happy with my question!"

Lizzy threw her arms around his neck and let her warm embrace give her answer. Pulling away from the man that she loved, Lizzy exclaimed, "Ah, Matt, being married to you is going to be better than all the money in the world!"

STOLEN KISSES : AN AMISH ROMANCE

124

MARISA MEYER

Chapter 1

Spring had awakened in the small Amish town, Mount Joy, birds were singing their spring interlude and blossoms covered the trees like frosting on a cake and the slight breeze carried its flowery sent through the village. But in the Fisher's home, it was the complete opposite. Rose Beiler's cousin Claire had gone into labour in the early hours of the morning and complications had set in. Somehow they had missed the fact she was pregnant with twins. One miracle baby had already been born and Rose was standing with the bundle in her arms while she looked on as the midwife tried her utmost to deliver the second one. Claire was in tremendous pain and agony and she had no more strength left to push.

"We need to get the Englisch doctor," Gretchen, the midwife said. Her voice desperate as she rubbed Claire's back where she lay on her side.

"And what would he do?" Rose's father muttered, standing with his straw hat in his hand.

Abraham Beiler had promised his sister on her death bed that he would protect Claire as if she was his own daughter, and with David, Claire's husband, having gone out of town, this was exactly what he was doing.

"The baby is not coming down, and it's in distress. He could do more than I can."

Rose watched her father tentatively. He was still very much old school, hated anything that represented the modern world and society. She could understand how he felt about cellular phones opening doors for evil to enter, but this was a matter of life and death. She adjusted the little baby's blanket and handed the child to the midwife.

"Daed, we cannot delay, if we don't call the Englisch doctor, Claire and the baby will die," she pleaded with her father. Her father studied her and a deep frown furrowed between his brows, the gentle touch of her hand on his arm brought his eyes to hers, "Please, we cannot lose Claire," she breathed.

"Fine!" he said frustrated, but his eyes were filled with concern.

Abraham was a muscular and tall man, people called him the Giant in jest because of his size, and although he may often come across as an intimidating individual, he had a soft heart. She knew that if he lost Claire because of his own stubbornness, he would never forgive himself, but sometimes he needed convincing.

Rose turned to her fiancé, Kemp, and nodded, "Go and hurry, Claire needs medical help urgently."

Kemp had been Rose's pillar of strength and from the age of sixteen it was a given that they would someday marry. It's been almost three years since he first made his intentions known and although their courtship had lasted a lot longer than most, she felt at ease and unburdened. She loved Kemp; he was a kind, generous and handsome man. Never had a harsh word to say and hardly ever got into any confrontations. Kemp also never said no whenever someone needed a helping hand. He was almost too good to be true.

Rose moved in next to her cousin and took her hand, "Hang in there, Kemp has gone to get the Englisch doctor, he will come and help."

Claire was incoherent and mumbled inaudibly, Rose sighed softly and said a silent prayer, then took a damp cloth to dab her cousin's feverish skin. Somewhere in the room the small cries of a newborn baby gave everyone a sparkle of hope. The midwife did everything possible to keep Claire comfortable while they waited for the doctor, but it felt as if time was in a suspended state.

An hour later, which felt like forever, Kemp burst into the kitchen and on his heels was the Englisch doctor, but it wasn't the doctor anyone expected.

"Where is Doctor Westbrook?" Abraham asked and looked out the door, half expecting him to come sauntering up the path.

"Good morning sir, I'm Dr Williams; unfortunately Dr Westbrook is at a conference in France..."

Abraham interrupted, "But you're so young."

Rose heard the commotion from the room and quickly got up to come and investigate and prevent Claire from getting too stressed.

She too was quite surprised when she got to the kitchen to find a strapping young man with a medical bag in his hand. Unlike Dr Westbrook who always arrived wearing his white coat, Dr Williams was dressed very casually, and she had to force herself to turn her attention back to the pressing matter.

"Daed, just let the doctor get on with it," Claire said and stood aside.

Dr Williams smiled confidently, "I can assure you Mr Beiler, I'm more than capable of assisting. Kemp mentioned that Claire is in labour?"

"Yah-yah, she is," Said Claire, wringing her hands nervously, "We did not know she was expecting twins. The midwife is with her, but she is not knowledgeable enough to help her."

Dr Williams nodded and skirted past Rose's father and nodded courteously at her. She glanced back at Kemp and Abraham. The concern etched on their faces matched hers. Two years ago they had buried her aunt, Claire's mother after she passed away due to pneumonia, and she knew that her father could not cope with another death in the family. *Be positive Rose*, she told herself before disappearing into the room and closing the door behind her. The less her father got to see, the better and until Claire was out of danger and the second infant was born, she would stay by her cousin's side. She just wishes David was here to support his wife.

David and Claire got married last fall, and although they looked like a happy couple on the outside, everything wasn't as peachy behind closed doors. When they first met, it wasn't a case of falling in love, it was an arranged betrothal, one Rose was opposed against, but everyone insisted that Claire marry before she turned thirty. Her mother had been overly concerned that she would end up becoming a spinster. When the bow finally broke and Claire agreed, she was introduced to David. He was from a neighbouring Amish community, only two days away by carriage. A few months after their marriage however, David kept making excuses to go back home, where he would stay for days at a time. No one else knew this, but Claire had told her that she suspected that David had another flame burning elsewhere, but it was not her place to make such accusations. Especially since David was the Bishop's son, so instead, Claire decided to simply turn a blind eye and hope it will all blow over one day.

Rose was convinced that all the stress and anxiety Claire had to deal with was the cause for her current predicament, and deep down she hated David for being so selfish. In the last few hours she had to repent more than once for feeling so angry towards him. Naturally, knowing how hard it had been for Claire to cope, she couldn't help but be nervous about her own engagement to Kemp. Especially since Kemp and David were friends. There was always that nagging voice in the back of her mind, asking her if he was really the right man for her and if she too, would one day become a lifeless bag of bones, living each day with no purpose.

No! She couldn't entertain these negative thoughts, Kemp was nothing like David she scolded herself and shook her head. Right now there were more important things at stake.

"When was the other baby born?" the doctor asked.

"About two hours ago," she said nervously.

"Did she have any difficulties with the birth?"

"I don't know Doctor, she gave birth, and it's not the easiest thing to do as is. What is wrong with her?"

He looked up at her and hooked his stethoscope in his ears and placed the end piece on Claire's abdomen; he listened tentatively and moved it around slowly. She couldn't help but notice the colour of his eyes. He had two different colour eyes, one hazel and one with a slight tinge of blue, which she found rather unusual. Again she had to remind herself to focus.

"Without a Caesarean section, the baby will not make it," he said and came around to look under the blanket.

"Is it that serious?" Rose asked, biting her lip.

"I'm afraid so, she's unconscious and in no position to give natural birth right now."

"Is she going to have to go to hospital?" Claire asked worriedly.

"There's no time," he said and moved around to his medical bag, "We will have to do it here."

"What!?" she cried out.

Rose's stomach bottomed out and her hand flew to her mouth, but his words were barely cold when her father stormed into the room demanding to know what was going on.

Rose calmed him down and get Kemp to take him outside while she stayed behind to assist. Everything had happened so fast, and a few minutes later, Claire's second baby was born healthy.

Chapter 2

Grant had known that Dr Westbrook had a special group of patients he did house calls to occasionally but what he didn't expect was for them to be Amish. When the guy on the carriage pulled up in front of the medical practice, he was rather intrigued, until he discovered why he had come.

What he knew of the Amish was what he had seen on TV and online, so when he arrived there he had no idea what he was in for. But he was pleasantly surprised. Other than Mr Beiler who was a little sceptic the others were rather pleasant. Kemp was a quiet individual, he only said what was needed and didn't bother to hold much conversation. The mid-wife clearly knew what she was doing; otherwise the other baby would have gone through the same trouble. And as for the girl, whose name he learned was Rose, she was a lot more verbal than the rest. She looked like the type who could take charge if the walls came tumbling down and throughout the procedure, she remained calm and collected, following his instructions to the T.

Both babies were healthy enough, not in need of medical attention. But Claire would need a few weeks to recover, which meant he would have make daily trips to Mount Joy to check on her. At least next time around he would drive here in his own car, which would probably take 10 minutes instead of an hour.

"Dr Williams," Rose said as he headed to the door.

"Yes Rose?"

"I just wanted to thank you for saving Claire and the baby today."

"You can call me Grant," he said and smiled, "It's what I'm there for."

"I know, but thank you anyway... Grant," she smiled appreciatively.

He nodded just as Kemp pushed past him to go outside so he stepped out of the man's way, and reached out to touch Rose's shoulder, "I'll be back tomorrow to check on them."

Rose flinched, and he immediately knew he had overstepped some sort of boundary. He really needed to brush up on Amish culture and understand the do's and do not's.

Chapter 2

The next day arrived with much promise and anticipation, Grant convinced himself that it was the mystery of this small Amish village that attracted him. It had nothing to do with the blue eyed woman in the plain purple dress and white apron, whose blonde hair was neatly tucked under her bonnet. For a moment while they worked to save the baby and Claire, he had wondered what she would look like with her hair loose.

As he drove into the small town, he was surprised to see far less people around than first expected. Compared to the day before, the town was almost half deserted and it was already past ten in the morning. Surely they would all be up and busy doing what Amish people do, by now. He pulled to a stop in front of the Beiler home and got out of his car. Even the house was quiet, and the curtains were still drawn. He contemplated waiting but as he turned to get back into his car, the front door opened.

"Dr Williams, I'm so sorry, I was busy helping Claire feed the babies."

His heart rate increased a fraction at the site of her and her half smile that caused the dimples in her cheeks to appear like wishing wells.

"Is it a convenient time or should I come back," he said. He had to remain professional. He was a doctor or heaven's sake.

"It's perfectly fine," said Rose and opened the door wider, "She's been resting, but the babies have been very restless."

Grant did whatever necessary to keep his mind focused on Claire and the babies, but with Rose hovering around like a mother hen protecting her chicks, he found it extra trying to concentrate.

"So how are you feeling Claire?" he asked, diverting his attention fully to his patient.

Claire flinched as she pushed herself up a little, "I'm fine, I'm so sorry you had to go through all the trouble to come out here."

"Oh don't apologize, it's what I do for a living, I'm just glad we saved both you and the baby. So have you named them yet?"

Claire shook her head and lowered her eyes, "No, I have to wait for my husband to return."

Rose snorted behind him, "David doesn't deserve you Claire."

"Rose! Don't talk like that." Claire looked at him, "David is a busy man, he will be here by the end of the week."

Grant noted immediately that Rose clearly did not like this David fellow, but again, it was not his place. He did however feel sorry for Claire having to have gone through this all on her own.

"And you Rose?" he asked casually not wanting to sound too fishy.

"What about me?"

"Do you have any children or a husband?"

There was a moment of silence and he looked up at her. She stood with her lips pursed and a slight frown etched on her forehead. Did he overstep again? He wondered.

"She's not married," Claire piped up.

"Claire!" Rosa reprimanded.

"What, it's the truth, you and Kemp have been courting, but nothing ever comes of it," Claire muttered and then reached to touch Grant's hand, "I think she's too afraid."

"What utter nonsense! I'm not afraid; I just don't see why I should rush anything."

Grant chuckled but didn't interject.

"What about you Doctor, are you married?"

"Oh for heaven's sake Clair, do you have to be so quizzical!" Rose reprimanded.

Grant smiled and shook his head, "I was married, but my wife is no longer alive, it's been almost four years."

"Oh goodness, I'm so sorry for your loss," Claire said with genuine sympathy.

Rose bit her lip and held her hand over her chest. The poor man must still grieve the loss of his wife and Claire is non-the-wiser.

Chapter 3

Rose was shocked that Claire would announce her status so carelessly, and of all things holy, what gave Dr Williams the right to ask such personal questions. She had stormed out of the room and stood waiting in the living room for him to finish what he came to do while pacing impatiently. What was it about this man? Since the day he walked into this house, there was this strange feeling of longing that suddenly rose up within her soul. It was as if she was missing something in her life, but she couldn't quite put her finger on it. Maybe it was seeing Claire in such peril that made her realize just how short life was, or maybe it was the miracle of birth. She was already nearing thirty and soon her father would pressurise her into marriage, and she was still not sure if it was what she wanted, and the arrival of the Englisch doctor didn't help her either.

She was just a little girl when she had found a little fox trapped in one of the fences that bordered Mount Joy. Her first instinct was to free the poor animal, which she did and since then she always wanted to help animals. She had discovered much later, that in order to be a Veterinarian, she would need to study, but that was against God's will. Or so her father said. *A woman's place is in the kitchen, caring for her husband and children,* her father had said countless times. But while she was still unmarried, she had the freedom to tend to the horses when the men were not around. A lot of the girls laughed at her and told her she was foolish, but she never let that get her down.

She twisted the string of her bonnet around her finger as she glanced out of the window and sighed. What if she was being foolish? Maybe it was time for her to settle down and start a family of her own.

"Rose?"

Grant's voice broke into her train of thought and she turned around.

"Claire is doing as well as expected, but I will have to come back again to make sure the incision does not become septic."

Rose nodded and walked to the door, her heart racing for no reason, "I will keep an eye on her too."

Grant walked to the door but before he exited the house, he stopped and faced her, "I didn't mean to pry into your life," he whispered.

She wanted to respond to that, but her brain and her lips were suddenly disconnected. She opened her mouth to speak but nothing came out. And then unexpectedly, Grant leaned forward and pressed his lips against hers. Rose froze instantly, her arms like steel against her sides but her insides were wreaking havoc. Her heart fluttered wildly in her chest and her stomach had filled with a kaleidoscope of butterflies, all flapping their colourful wings at once.

When Grant raised his head, and the moment had passed, she slowly opened her eyes and looked into his deep soulful eyes.

"I-I'm sorry, I shouldn't have done that," he said immediately. He raised his hand as if to touch her cheek but withdrew it as if the contact would burn his fingers.

Realization swept over Rose followed by an immense feeling of guilt. She had just allowed an Englisch man to kiss her, and that while she was promised to another. Without a word she almost shoved him out the door and slammed the door shut. How could she have allowed herself to be so foolish! She had committed an adulterous sin and for that she knew she was going to be punished. But even then she could still feel the warmth of his lips on hers, and it felt so right, and so natural.

The sound of his car drifted further and further away, and only once she could no longer hear it, did she peek out of the window. Thankfully there were very few people in town this morning since they had all gone to a barn raising. She was horrified at the thought of what would happen had anyone witnessed what had just happened. She brought her trembling fingers to her lips and she let out a sigh.

"Rose!" Claire called from the room.

Rose took a deep steadying breath, fixed her bonnet and raised her chin. No one needed to know what happened, and when the doctor comes again, she would make sure she was not around. After all, she never returned the kiss.

"Do you need anything?" she asked her cousin.

"Dr Williams is a great man," she said and Rose swallowed.

"He is handy to have around," she mumbled.

"He likes you."

Rose's eyes grew as wide as saucers and she regarded her cousin, "He's Englisch, just because he asked me about my status, doesn't mean he likes me," she muttered.

"I saw the way he looked at you."

"He probably looks at every woman like that."

"Not the way he looked at you, he was taken by you."

Rose threw her hands up and shook her head, "Why are we having this conversation? Even if he liked me, you know very well that it's futile, he's not Amish. Besides, I'm happily engaged to a wonderful man, thank you very much."

Claire reached for Rose's hand and squeezed it, "Don't make the same mistakes I made, just look where that has gotten me."

Rose bent down and brushed a stray strand of hair from her cousin's face, "It's gotten you two beautiful children, and maybe, just maybe by God's grace, this is the exact thing David needs to realize what an amazing wife he has."

Claire's eyes shot full of tears and she shook her head, "No, that will never change. Maybe if we had met without the intervention of the bishop and we let things advance naturally, there would have been hope, but David does not love me. He tolerates the notion of marriage and respects the faith."

"Oh Claire," Rose said and carefully hugged her cousin, "God works in mysterious ways, he would not have put you two together was it not His will."

Claire didn't reply, simply sniffed and then plastered a brave smile on her face, "At least you and Kemp got to know each other."

"Exactly, so I'm very happy with my engagement and there's no reason for my eyes to wander to a certain doctor simply because he's handsome."

Claire laughed wholeheartedly, "So you do think he's handsome!"

"There's no denying that!"

The two women spent the rest of the morning talking about life, Rose helped Claire to feed the twins and she bathed and dressed them and saw to nappy changes. It kept her mind busy to say the least, and for the time being she forced herself not to pay a single thought of Dr Williams.

Chapter 4

It was a lovely spring morning, and like every other morning so far, Grant was getting ready to head out to Mount Joy to see to his patient. He was about to leave when his receptionist announced that he had a visitor.

"Send him in," he said and put down the receiver.

It was Kemp who entered the rooms and although Grant was poised and calm, his insides were in a knot.

"Kemp, what brings you to town?" he asked casually.

Kemp took his hat off and clutched it in front of him, "Dr Williams, I'm sorry to barge in like this, but I was wondering if I may have a word with you?"

Uh-oh, Grant thought as he gestured for Kemp to take a seat. First thing that crossed his mind was the kiss, what if Kemp had seen it?

"So what can I do for you?" he asked curiously.

Kemp cleared his throat and sat down, "You know about the Amish yah?"

Grant nodded not sure where this was going, "A little, but not much, why?"

"Well, in the Amish, men may not study, if they do, they have to leave the community, which means they will be shunned."

Confused, Grant leaned forward on his elbows and regarded the man in front of him, "So if you want to further your education you are not allowed to?"

He nodded his head and looked down, "The thing is, I want to do what you do, I want to be a doctor and as long as I am at Mount Joy, I can't realize my dream."

Grant studied the man and he could understand exactly how conflicted he must be, "So if you decide to study, you cannot go back to Mount Joy?"

Kemp shook his head, "Yah, I can go back, but I will be like you, Englisch, I won't be able to partake in certain things, and I won't be able to marry Rose. But you see, Rose and I..."

The rest of the conversation was muted by Grant's own thoughts at realizing that Kemp was Rose' fiancé and just yesterday, he had so boldly overstepped his welcome by kissing her.

"... she will understand," Kemp said and sat back.

Grant hadn't heard a single word he was saying and shifted awkwardly in his chair.

"How do you think she would feel?" he shot in the dark.

"Rose is a strong woman, I care for her greatly but she will not stand in my way if I wish to become a doctor."

This was just too overwhelming, he thought. If Kemp was considering leaving behind everything he knew that meant he would leave Rose behind too. There was a flutter of excitement in his insides and he sat steeping his fingers together.

"I think you need to speak to Rose and tell her exactly how you feel."

Kemp nodded and then stood up, "That is what I intend to do."

Later that same day, Grant had visited Claire, but Rose was nowhere to be seen. Worried that Kemp may have spoken to her, to tell her about his plans and how she would take it, he had very nonchalantly asked Clair where she was. She was also not sure where her cousin was, but told him to wait around if he wanted to see her. He didn't, it was far too awkward, not knowing head or tail how Rose felt. He too, had some conflict, after his wife Angelique died of leukaemia he vowed never to marry again. He had loved his wife almost more than life itself and what was the hardest part of all was the fact that despite his qualifications as a medical doctor, he could do nothing about the disease that claimed his wife's life. So naturally, these feelings that started out of nowhere for a woman he hardly knew was just as much a surprise as the fact that he was falling for an Amish woman.

Over the next week or two, Grant made regular trips to the town and slowly got to know more and more of the community, occasionally he saw Rose, and although he yearned to talk to her, he couldn't bring himself to do so. She was like that breath of fresh air, a city boy needed, to get a new lease on life, but she was indefinitely out of his reach.

Kemp was also still around, and it didn't look like he had made any effort to talk to Rose about his feelings towards studying further, which led him to believe that Kemp was going to simply stay put and submit to the laws of his kin.

Chapter 5

A month had passed, and Grant was still a regular visitor to Mount Joy, the resident doctor, the community dubbed him. But every day it had become harder and harder for Rose to cope. Her father was pressing her to decide and marry Kemp. But every time she laid eyes on Grant, she knew beyond the shadow of a doubt that she couldn't marry Kemp, not while her heart was torn in two.

It was one morning when she went to collect eggs from the chicken coop that she stole some time for herself. She needed God to guide her and help her make the right choices. She needed Him to rid her of these feelings of desire and guilt. She placed the egg basket on one of the crates and knelt down.

"Almighty God and Heavenly Father, you who know everyone's heart and failings, and who know the secrets we keep hidden, I ask you to help and comfort, and I beg you for guidance during this time. Forgive me my sins, which I have committed against you in word or deed, knowingly or unknowingly. I pray this in Your Holy name. Amen."

She had just gotten up off her knees when she heard a noise outside the coop and she went to investigate, it was Kemp and David, who had eventually returned to help Claire with the children. Afraid that they would notice her, she stayed hidden behind the wooden wall.

"I want to leave this place," she heard Kemp say.

"And go where?" asked David.

"I spoke to the Englisch doctor, I told him that I wanted to study further and also become a doctor."

Rose couldn't believe her ears, with her hand cupped over her mouth to quieten her breaths; she listened tentatively as Kemp told David that he was not ready to settle down. David warned him of the consequences of his actions too, but Kemp already had his heart set on leaving the Amish community, not so much the faith, but just to explore the world and find a bigger purpose.

Her heart ached in her chest, because like him, she always wanted to be a woman of purpose, not a simple girl working in the kitchen and seeing to a man's every need. Perhaps, this was the sign God had sent her, she thought quietly and waited for the two men to leave again. But even if this was a sign that she was not to be married now, what good would that do? She could still not consider the Englisch doctor, it was and absurd notion to say the least, and her father would have a cadenza. She was undoubtedly still stuck between a rock and a hard place, but at least it was a step closer to freedom. As soon as the two men left, she hurried to collect all the eggs, but as she stepped out of the chicken coop, the very object of her desire came walking across the field towards her. She stopped in her tracks, and even considered throwing the eggs at him to keep him away from her, but that would be silly.

"Rose, Claire told me I could find you here," he called with that heart stopping smile tugging at the corners of his lips.

"I was collecting eggs, is Claire all right?" she asked curiously.

"She's fine," he said as he stopped in front of her, "I wanted to apologise to you."

"What for?" *Apologise for the kiss or for falling into my life so unexpectedly, or for causing me to doubt my place in the Amish faith?* Her thoughts rallied.

"The kiss, I was completely out of line, and I wanted to apologise for my behaviour," he said as he crossed his arms over his chest, "I swear to you that I haven't told a single soul and I would never disgrace you."

She was surprised by his actions, but more so, she questioned them. Was he apologizing because he no longer desired her, or because he came to his senses and realized that there could be nothing between them?

"I forgive you," she simply said and gathered her skirt before sweeping past him like a gentle breeze.

"Rose..." he said, and she stopped.

"I-I don't regret it, and if I had another chance, I would do it again. You are a beautiful woman."

She felt her cheeks heat up, and she lowered her gaze, avoiding eye contact was the only thing that would keep her from dropping the eggs and running into his arms to just have one more kiss. She didn't respond to his admission though, instead, she turned and headed back towards the house, but all the while she could feel his eyes on her.

At dinner, Rose, Claire, David and Abraham sat quietly at the table; there was an eerie silence in the room.

"Is everything okay uncle?" Claire asked curiously.

"All is well," Abraham said as he poked around his plate.

Claire gave a shrug and continued eating, but Rose couldn't ignore the dreadful feeling of hopelessness that filled her insides.

"Kemp is leaving Mount Joy," Abraham said after a while, and both Claire and Rose gasped, and although Rose already knew, the finality of it came as a shock.

"He's leaving?" Claire uttered.

"Yah," David said, "He wants to study further."

Her father nodded and reached for Rose's hand, "You will find another suitor my child, if this is God's will then so be it, do not let it trouble you."

"But why didn't he tell me in person?" she asked, feigning disappointment.

"He couldn't bear hurting you, he left earlier today, but he told me to tell you that he'll always care for you," said David and dug into the potatoes.

"But we were going to marry!" Rose objected, placing her knife and fork down on the table.

"Only if God willed it," Abraham said and then continued with his meal, "The Lord, clearly has other plans for you."

Rose glanced towards Claire whose mouth was still gaping, and instead of being heartbroken she smiled at Claire, who raised an amused brow.

"I suppose it's for the best then," Claire breathed and reached for Rose's hand, "You'll find a wonderful husband yet."

Rose smiled and thanked God silently for hearing a part of her prayer at least. It had brought another season of freedom, which meant she could come and go as she pleased without the noose of marriage; to a man she cared for but didn't truly love, hanging around her neck.

As Claire got up to clear the dishes, Abraham cleared his throat, "Oh and another thing, the Englisch doctor decided to embrace the

Amish faith, and the Bishop agreed that he can continue his practice here and serve the community."

Claire dropped a plate, and it shattered on the floor and Rose nearly leaped off of her chair with excitement, but she stayed calm and collected.

"Well that's just brilliant! We could use the skill of a qualified doctor around here," Claire exclaimed as she started cleaning up her mess.

Abraham nodded, "Indeed, after what you had to endure, it didn't take much to convince the elders."

"Isn't that wonderful Rose?" Claire exclaimed but Rose simply nodded and smiled awkwardly.

In the back of the house, the wail of the twins echoed and David and Claire rushed to attend to the hungry infants.

Chapter 6

Grant stood on the porch outside of his new home in Mount Joy; he had made a brave move to adopt the Amish faith. Not only because he secretly hoped to win the hand of Rose Beiler, but because something deep down evoked a feeling a desire to have a more substantial connection with God. The realisation that he had lost his faith came as unexpectedly as his growing feelings for Rose. All his life he had worked towards saving lives, treating illnesses and being the prophet of doom for telling families that their loved ones had passed away. And when his wife died, he somehow blamed God. It was at that time that he realized just how insignificant life really was. In the end all the knowledge he had gained and practiced could save some lives, but it could never save souls. Raised in a Christian home, he had the foundation of faith, but never really lived it. But ever since visiting this community, and as days turned into weeks and he got to spend more time with these people, he started to slowly realise that he needed to choose for the sake of his soul.

His first day as an Amish community member, had come to an end and although he was yet to be baptised, the folk were treating him like one of their own and he couldn't have asked for anything better. He was about to turn in for the evening when Rose came walking up the small path to his house and his heart thrummed in his chest.

"Good evening Rose," he said and smiled.

"Evening to you Grant, I just came to bring you some dinner. It was Claire's idea."

Grant chuckled and took the dish from Rose, "Well, your cousin clearly knows when a man needs to be fed."

Rose laughed softly and tucked a strand of hair behind her ear, "Indeed she does, anyway, may the Lord bless you."

She turned to leave, but Grant stopped her, "Do you want to have dinner with me?" he asked.

Rose laughed and shook her head, "I don't think that would be appropriate," she said but then turned and looked at him, "Maybe once you're baptised, you can offer me a ride in your buggy to a sing gathering, or to one of the church services."

Grant studied her and smirked, "Are you playing hard to get?"

"I'm playing by the rules," she said and smiled.

Grant held back the urge to pull her into his arms and silently thanked God that he had a dish in his hands, "I think I need to get my hands on the rule book and familiarise myself with these customs."

Rose laughed and swept down and plucked a small Daisy from the flower pot on the porch, "That would be wise notion doctor," she whispered and smiled before laying the daisy on top of the dish he held in his hands.

"Wise indeed, so do you promise to let me take you to the church service once I have been baptised?" he asked teasingly.

"Only if you promise to behave," she joked.

"I swear on my life," he chuckled.

~*~

A few months later, Rose stood outside the house, with Claire peeking through the window ever two minutes. Her heart was beating out of control as she waited for Grant to arrive. He had finally been baptised and although it was almost impossible to stay away from him, she managed to do so by the grace of God and hours of praying and fasting.

When Grant finally arrived, and he got out of the buggy, he grinned and walked up the stairs to meet her.

"It's been a trying time for me," he whispered as he looked down at her.

"But worth the wait?" she teased.

Grant smiled and moved his hand from behind his back holding a single Daisy in his hand, "Would you do me the honour of allowing me to take you to church?"

From inside the house, Rose could hear Claire squeal with delight and she couldn't help but laugh.

"I would be delighted," she whispered and gently took the daisy from him and placed it in her bible.

Genesis 2:18 The LORD God said, "It is not good for the man to be alone. I will make a helper suitable for him."

An amish surprise

ABBY BARKER

Alison sat at the large pine desk in her father's study looking over the month's finances for her family's carriage shop. At twenty-years-old she had a womanly appearance in all things but her height. Her legs dangling from the seat, she looked almost like a child playing pretend at daddy's desk, but the work she did was certainly not childlike or imaginary. Alison had been helping run the family business for as long as she could write coherent sentences.

Ever since she was small, her parents noticed that their eldest daughter had a penchant for picking up new skills. When it came time to learn their multiplication tables in school, Alison had the entire thing memorized by the end of the week. When her father brought her to carriage shop to show her how the buggies were made it only took one quick look at the thing before she picked up a wrench and started putting it together herself. The unknown never frightened Alison, it only challenged her.

Over time, she went from touring the shop to unofficially running it alongside her father. Her parents never had a son, just Alison and her younger sister Emily, so there was no question as to who would take over the family business. And even if she did have a brother, Alison's father confided in her, there was no way he could do a better job.

Alison remembered her father's pride at times like these. One of their employees had consistently misreported the sales made during his shift. Alison had to flip through the book, page by page, to find his mistakes and correct them. She had made it halfway through when her father came into the study.

"My dear, it's a beautiful Saturday morning. I appreciate that you're doing but it's okay to take a break every once in a while."

"Papa, if I don't do this now we'll have twice as much work to do come Monday. Isaac skewed all the numbers with his carelessness. If I don't correct it, who will?"

"I will! Alison, you're not running the carriage shop on your own quite yet. Don't forget that this is our family's business, not just Alison's business."

"I know, Papa. You're right, but I'd rather get this finished so I can enjoy the rest of my Saturday instead of dwelling on it all weekend."

Her father sighed. He knew it was no use arguing with his daughter after she sets her mind to something. She was even more stubborn than he was.

"Okay, but when you're through please do join us outside. Your sister's cooked up a delicious lunch for us all. She set up a lovely picnic in the yard!"

Alison mumbled a response without looking up from her work. Her father smiled amusingly at his daughter and left the room. Sometimes she wondered if she'd be better off acting more like Emily. Alison loved her sister but she was a simple girl. She had always been content with living the life of a traditional Amish girl and was downright excited to become a traditional Amish woman. Alison wanted to get married, to start a family, and to raise that family Amish, but she wanted all of that without having to give up running the family business. While her father supported her decision, the rest of their community – including her own mother – thought her to be a little *too* ambitious.

"How could she balance the responsibility of raising children with a business?" the women at church would Alison's mother. "A mother's business is her children. She doesn't need both."

The never spoke that way about Emily. Emily was a good Amish girl: her only goals were to find a good Amish man to marry so they could start a good Amish family together. The simplicity of it all bored Alison to even think about. Why shouldn't she want more? It was her life, after all.

Alison finished the last page of corrections and readied herself to join her family outside. Her father was right it was a beautiful day.

A slight breeze rustled the prairie grass that surrounded her family's home and the sun warmed her skin. Her mother and father sat on a colorful quilt spread out on the lawn while Emily carried dishes of food out from the kitchen. She almost ran Alison right of the porch on her focused quest to deliver a loaf of bread to their parents.

"Oh! Alison, I didn't see you there. In fact, I this is the first time I've seen you all day. I thought you might still be sulking in Papa's study."

"I wasn't sulking, Emily, I was working. I know you've at least heard of the word."

"No need to be salty just because I know how to enjoy my Saturday. Now, when you're ready to stop being so uptight feel free to join us on the lawn."

Alison huffed, but followed Emily out to the picnic anyways. Emily had no right to tell her to relax, but she wasn't wrong. It couldn't hurt to spend a couple hours with her family before getting back to work. Papa fed Mama a cube of cheese while Mama giggled before either of them realized that their daughters had returned to the picnic. Alison felt a pang of longing in her stomach for a relationship like the one her parents had. The simplicity of it all felt almost unattainable for someone like her.

"Whoops! Didn't see you there, girls. Your mother was just enjoying a little cheese."

Alison's mother smiled sheepishly behind the dainty hand that covered her mouth.

"Don't mind us! I was just bringing out some bread to go along with it and Alison finally decided to crawl out of her cave to join us."

"Ha-ha, very funny Emily. Let's all make jokes about Alison the Hard-Working Cave Troll."

"I never said you were a troll, just that you live in a cave."

"Girls, please, neither of you are trolls. All right? Please stop going out of your ways to upset each other."

Both girls begrudgingly nodded in agreement. Alison tore a hunk of bread from the loaf to fill her mouth with something other than a rebuttal to her sister's joke. Emily appeared to have moved on almost instantly, chattering on about some new recipe or another that she learned from a friend of hers in town.

"And Mama, she says you absolutely must add a dash of paprika to the marinade. It truly makes the meal."

It was truly the most boring conversation Alison had ever sat in on. As much as she tried she just could not find an interest in cooking. One of the main tenants of being a good wife was completely and utterly dull to her. How could anyone possibly expect her to live a fulfilling life the traditional way when so much of it left her unfulfilled? She pushed these thoughts away as to not mar the nice time she was having with her family. It really was nice she had to admit.

When Emily wasn't being a bratty little sister she was actually a very poised and charismatic young woman. What she lacked in intelligence, she made up for in charm. It was a characteristic that she definitely inherited from their mother when Alison apparently passed up on it. Not to say Alison wasn't charming in her own way, just not in the same immediately obvious sense that Emily was. It was the kind of thing that caused neighbors to ask their mother, "How's Emily?" before following up with, "Oh, yes, I almost forgot, and Alison?" This almost never truly bothered Alison, but when it did she would just burry herself in work until the feeling passed.

"Lights of my life, I'm going to head into town soon to pick a very special surprise for us all. Don't bother asking me what it is, I won't tell you. I only bring it up to ask if there's anything else you might need while I'm out."

"Oh Papa, a surprise? You must tell us! I don't know if I can wait."

"I'm sorry Emily, you'll just have to be patient. But, believe me, it will be worth the wait."

Emily squealed with joy and threw herself down on the lawn. Quite a spectacle for some unknown present, Alison thought. She'd wait until after she learned what the surprise is before offering up an appropriate response.

"Thank you, Papa. I'm sure whatever it is will be lovely. Would you mind, while you're there, picking up some more pencils? I've about worn mine all down to a nub fixing all of Isaac's mistakes."

"Of course, my little busy bee. Even after hearing that you'll be getting a life-changing surprise you're still thinking about work. I don't know whether to be impressed or to try fruitlessly once again to enjoy a day off."

"Don't bother. She's about as close to enjoying herself as you are to telling us what the surprise is."

"I am enjoying myself. Has it ever occurred to you that I enjoy working?"

"Of course you enjoy working. That's because you don't have an exciting bone in your entire body!"

"Girls! That's enough. You're father is planning something very special for us and the least you two can do is spend a moment with us without bickering. Do you think you can do that?"

"Yes, Mama," they said in unison.

The little family spent the rest of the afternoon playing games on the lawn, chatting about the family business, and all around enjoying each other's company. Alison even let Emily braid ribbons into her hair, which she promptly removed at the first chance she got. They tried to spend time all together like this at least once a week. Papa valued family time above most else. He enjoyed running the carriage shop, but only because a successful business meant he could provide for his family. He lived for moments like these when he could simply watch the three most important people in his life sit happily in the sun.

Papa kissed each of his girls on the cheeks before taking their buggy into town. Alison immediately retreated into the study, while Mama and Emily began preparing for dinner. He said he wouldn't be long; surprising them was just as exciting as being surprised. It wasn't until after the sunset and the food began to get cold did they start to worry.

"It's getting awfully late. Shouldn't Papa be back by now?"

"Don't worry, dear. He probably just got caught up preparing whatever it is he wanted to surprise us with. You know how elaborate your father's plans can get."

Their father did have a tendency to overdo things, like the time they had to repaint the barn so he chose the loudest, brightest blue he could find. You could practically see the barn from space. Papa was so proud of the color that Mama couldn't help but put aside her fears of what the neighbors might say. But Alison had a sinking feeling in her stomach. A minute later there was a knock on the door. The three women sat at the kitchen table for a moment before Alison stood up to answer it. On the other side was a small, nervous looking man. She recognized him as the owner of the local general store. She took one look at his face and knew exactly what he was about to tell her.

"Evening Miss Raber. Are your mother and sister home, too?"

"Please, what happened to my father? Just tell me."

"He had a heart attack, miss. Right in my shop. He collapsed onto the floor and I sent my daughter straight away to fetch the doctor, but when he arrived was nothing he could do. I'm so sorry to be the one to tell you this, but it happened in my store, you see, and I feel that it's the least I can do."

"Papa's dead?" Emily wailed.

Mama laid her head in her hands and didn't make a sound, but Alison didn't react at all.

"The doctor said to tell you to come by in the morning to discuss arrangements. Oh, and these were in his hand when he collapsed."

The shop owner handed Alison a bundle of pencils.

"Thank you very much. Have a pleasant evening."

Alison mechanically shut the door and returned to the kitchen table, pencils clutched in her fist. Emily sobbed and muttered incoherently but Alison could barely hear her. Outwardly, she showed no emotion, but inside her entire world had been flipped upside down. She had thought about what life might be like without her father before, but it was always years in the future, sometimes decades. She'd be middle aged with a husband and a couple children, ready to take over managing the carriage shop completely on her own. They would have prepared for this day as he got older. He would have had time to pass on everything he knew about running a business, and more importantly, running a family. Now she'd never know any of that.

Her father was the one person in Alison's life that supported her one hundred percent of the time. Whether she wanted a family or not, to run the family business or not, he was on her side. She loved her mother, but Mama just didn't understand her like Papa did. In this moment, she felt completely alone.

"I wonder what the surprise was."

"Alison, how can you think of that at a time like this?" Mama spoke up for the first time. Emily cried even harder.

"We're going to have a lot to do in the morning. I think I'll go to bed and get some rest."

Alison didn't mean to be callous. She had never been good at sharing her emotions with other people, even her family. She needed to take some time to herself to process what had happened.

On the way to her room she remembered the first time her father let her drive the family buggy. He had built the buggy with his own hands a couple years before. His father passed down the skill, just as his grandfather had done before. The only thing Papa was more proud of than his buggy was his family. Whenever something broke, no matter how problematic, there was never a question as to whether or not they should fix it or replace it. Eventually, Papa started teaching Alison how to repair the trusty old thing and then how to drive it soon after.

She was accompanying him into town one day to pick up some supplies for Mama's garden when he scooted over on the bench and threw Alison the reigns.

"You're in charge now! I'm going to take a quick nap. Wake me up when we're in town."

He leaned back in his seat, crossed his arms behind his head and closed his eyes. Alison was startled at first, but instinct quickly took over. She shied away from people, but never a challenge. Although Papa only pretended to close his eyes, Alison reacted as if he had given her complete control of the vehicle. She applied all of the knowledge she had about making and repairing the carriage, as well as her experience riding horses, to steering it. She didn't so much as hit a bump in the road and navigated them straight into town. Her father pretended to wake up from his nap with an exaggerated yawn.

"What did I miss? Are we there yet?"

He constantly challenged her and never underestimated her and maybe that was what he was doing now. She wasn't prepared to lose him so soon, but that didn't mean she couldn't handle it. It was just like learning to drive, except this time after he tossed her the reigns and leaned back in his seat he closed his eyes for good.

In the morning, Alison woke up to the familiar smell of brewing coffee and baking bread. In the kitchen she found Emily cooking silently at the stove. She turned to smile at Alison when she heard her walk in. Alison noticed that her eyes were ringed with red.

"Good morning, Alison. Would you like a cup of coffee?"

"Yes, that would be nice. Thank you," she took a seat at the table. "Where's Mama?"

"Still sleeping I suppose."

Her sister's faux-cheerful tone had Alison worried. Whereas she kept her emotions constantly under wraps, Emily wore her heart on her sleeve. It wasn't like her to feign any sort of emotion, especially when it was so obviously false.

"Emily, are you alright?"

"Yes, of course. It's a lovely morning, isn't it?"

"Emily. Do you remember what happened last night?"

"Of course, silly. Papa went to the store and had a heart attack and is gone forever so now I'm doing everything I can to distract myself from that memory because it's just too terrible for me to bear. Cream and sugar?"

"I'm sorry, Emily. I just...you were acting so strangely."

"Strange? What about you? You barely said a word last night and just went straight to bed like that man just showed up on our doorstep to deliver your pencils instead of the news that our father is dead! You acted like some kind of emotionless robot."

"Just because I wasn't blubbering uncontrollably like you doesn't mean I wasn't upset."

"Well, just because I'm smiling now doesn't mean I'm not upset either."

Emily slammed a cup of coffee on the table in front of Alison and turned back to the stove. Mama shuffled into the kitchen just in time to cut through the tense silence. She walked up behind Alison, squeezed her shoulders, and kissed her on the top of her head before walking over to Emily and hugging her from behind.

"My darling girls, I love you both very, very much. Never doubt that."

"We know, Mama. We love you too. Coffee?"

It looked as if it took a great effort for her to nod her head.

"Mama, I'll go into to town today to talk to the doctor. You should stay in and rest. Emily will take care of you."

Mama smiled sadly, "Thank you, sweetheart. I think I'll do just that. You really are your father's daughter, taking charge in even the darkest moments. I'm proud of you."

"Thanks, Mama."

Alison kissed her mother on the cheek and got ready to go into town. Someone had brought their buggy back home last night there was at least one thing she didn't have to worry about. Alison hitched the horses up and set off.

She knew the way to the doctor's office quite well. It's where they would go when Emily had a fever that wouldn't break or when Alison cut her hand open working in the carriage shop. But those things could all be fixed with a few stitches or a prescription. She'd never been there for anything as untreatable as death.

Doctor Miller greeted Alison with a pitying smile.

"Alison, I am so sorry for your family's loss. Your father was a great man and beloved member of our community."

She could tell that it was the same spiel he gave every grieving family member who walked through his doors. Never the less, she thanked him for his condolences. They spoke about funeral arrangements and cause of death. He brought up grief counseling but she denied it. After they finished and he once again told her how sorry he was for her loss, Alison decided to stop by the general store to thank the shop owner once again and apologize for slamming the door in his face.

Standing outside of the shop was a lanky but handsome young man leaning near the door. She was surprised she didn't recognize him. It wasn't often that an unfamiliar face showed up in their small town. He turned to look her in the eyes when he noticed her approaching, which even more surprisingly, made Alison blush. A frame of long lashes softened his dark brown eyes. She didn't know this man, but those eyes made her feel like she could trust him.

"You! Are you one of the Raber girls?"

This man was full of surprises.

"Oh, well, yes, I am. And who might you be?"

"Nathan. Nathan Fisher. I knew your father. Forgive me, but which sister are you?"

"Alison."

"Ah, the first born."

How much did her father tell this man?

"You knew my father? How do I not know you then?"

"I guess I didn't know him well. Just well enough for him to describe his daughters to me in great detail," he flashed her a coy grin. "I'm sure we would have met sooner or later."

"I see, but *how* do you know my father?"

"I'm your surprise!"

The blush across Alison's cheeks brightened.

"Well, not really, but I have your surprise. When your father never showed up to collect it yesterday I went asking for him and learned what had happened. I'm truly sorry."

The way he looked at her when he said those words assured her that it wasn't just a canned sentiment from a stranger. He meant every word and she felt comforted by it. How could a brief exchange with a stranger relieve her, even slightly, from the pain she felt when not even her family members could do the same?

"Thank you, Nathan. That's very kind of you to say."

"I thought if I waited around here long enough, one of you would show up and I could make sure you received your father's gift. I could have asked around as to where you lived and brought it directly to you, but I didn't want to intrude. If you don't mind me saying, I didn't expect it find you out and about so soon. Your composure in all this is admirable."

"Someone must be strong for my mother and sister."

"And who will be strong for you?"

Alison was taken aback by the question. Nathan quickly realized that he might have overstepped his boundaries.

"Forgive me once again. I can't begin to know what you're going through."

"No, it's alright. I just haven't really had time to stop and think about me yet."

"You're very brave, Alison. I know I've only just met you but I already think so."

She smiled down at her feet. Alison had never spoken to someone so sincere, especially not upon meeting them for the first time.

"Anyway, I've got this gift for you and your family that I'd like to deliver. I can hold on to it for as long as you'd like, but I think you'd enjoy it."

"What is it?"

"I can't tell! I promised your father that you wouldn't know what it is until it landed on your doorstep and I intend to keep that promise."

"Well then, can you come by tomorrow around midday? We'll all be home then."

"Absolutely, Alison Raber. I'd be delighted to."

Alison relished his genuine lightheartedness. Her own natural callousness coupled with Emily's shame happiness had made for a difficult twenty-four hours. Nathan seemed to know exactly when to be somber and when to joke around and had the ability to flow seamlessly between them. After she told him where she lived and softly touched her on the shoulder when he said goodbye, Alison hoped that tomorrow wouldn't be the last time she would see Nathan Fisher.

He arrived at their home right before lunchtime the next day. Instead of a buggy, Nathan pulled up in a worn-down pickup truck. Alison was sitting on the porch reading when he arrived.

"Why, hello Miss Raber!" he yelled from the window, waving one hand frantically in the air. "I have your delivery."

It was then that she noticed the happy golden retriever leaning his head over the back of the truck. Nathan jumped out of the car, walked around to the back, and opened the hatch. Out jumped the excited dog followed by a miniature version of her. Both dogs immediately rushed onto the porch to great Alison.

"Let me introduce you to Maeve and her son No-Name."

"No-Name?"

"He's your surprise! It didn't feel right naming him myself so I've been calling him No-Name for the time being. You and your sister get to name him, and your Mama if she'd like to chime in."

"Papa got us a puppy?"

"A purebred farm dog! My lady Maeve had puppies a handful of weeks ago and I put up fliers in the area letting people know they were up for adoption. Your father got in contact with me and handpicked little No-Name here just for you. He said, 'My girls deserve to love something that will always love them back, other than me of course.' Your pa had a right sense of humor, kept me laughing every time he came to check up on the little guy."

"And how often was that?"

"Oh, at least once a week or so. He'd come over and sit with Maeve and the pups for at least an hour. He wanted to make sure he was getting the right dog for his daughters. We'd chat the entire time. Got to know quite a bit about him and you ladies over time."

"Oh yeah? Like what?" Alison asked, only half fighting to push away the barrage of doggy kisses Maeve and No-Name were laying on her.

"That your mother was the love of his life until you and your sister came along. He told me that Emily is the youngest, but the most outgoing person he'd ever met. He called her 'sunshine on a rainy day.' And you, Miss Raber, he said you were really something else."

"Something else? Is that all he said?"

"Oh, I think that says everything I need to know, don't you?"

Was he teasing her? The smile on his face seemed to say so. Alison was just about to rebuttal when Emily came squealing out of the house.

"Puppies! Mama, come quickly! A pair of pooches have come to pay us a visit."

Emily threw herself on the ground near the two excited dogs. They quickly moved their attention from Alison to cover her with affection. Emily laughed for the first time since her father's passing and the musical sound lit up the entire yard. Alison mustered a smile, warmed by her sister's joy, but Nathan responded with a full on guffaw.

"That laugh could make a mean old grizzly bear smile! I'm glad you like them Miss Emily because the little one's yours."

Emily gasped and scooped No-Name up into her arms.

"You mean it? We get to keep him?"

"Yup! He's your surprise!"

She held the pup tighter and tears welled up in her eyes. Alison noticed and started to feel emotional as well. The two girls were touched by their father's love as if he were currently there with them. Not wanting to show her feelings, Alison quickly changed the subject.

"Emily, this is Nathan Fisher. Papa answered one of his ads about puppies for sale a few weeks ago. He picked out little No-Name just for us."

"No-Name?"

"That's what I've been calling him since I didn't think it would be fair of me to name him before ya'll got a chance, but your father had another name for him. I don't think he meant for me to hear it but sometimes I caught him whispering to the little guy and calling him 'Angel.'"

"Angel! Oh, Alison we must name him Angel. It's what Papa would have wanted. Plus, he's our little Angel come to look over us. It's perfect."

Angel was a perfect name for the pup, almost too perfect. If it was only up to her she'd probably keep calling him No-Name, but for the sake of keeping the peace she agreed with her sister.

"Angel is a perfect name. That's what we'll call him. For Papa."

Mama finally emerged from the house to see what all the fuss was about. Angel wriggled free from Emily's arms to say "hello" to her. He jumped up to her knees and pawed at her skirt.

"Oh my! Who is this adorable creature?"

"That's Angel, Mama! He's Papa's surprise."

Mama picked up the squirming puppy and held him gently in her arms. She cooed softly and rocked him back and forth with tears in her eyes. The rambunctious pup calmed down for the first time since arriving and gave her one small lick on the cheek. The tender moment was difficult for Alison to watch. It wasn't easy to see her mother's vulnerability on display, especially in front of a practical stranger. Nathan realized this, too, and attempted to excuse himself.

"Well, I'm happy to have been the messenger of some joy in this unfortunate time of your lives. Maeve and I will be on our way now. I can see No-Name, I mean Angel, is in good hands."

"Don't be silly! You must stay for lunch, you and Maeve. It's the least we can do to thank you for this wonderful gift."

"I didn't do much. It's your husband's gift after all, but I'll graciously accept a meal and some time to spend with the wonderful women I've heard so much about."

Alison was flooded with emotions. Her father's passing, a puppy appearing on their doorstep, Nathan's unending charm. She had been so distracting focusing on the business half of her life plan that she had almost forgotten about the relationship part. And now she had met this man, albeit under complicated circumstances, that made her heart skip a beat. She didn't want to get ahead of herself, in fact she didn't know if she was capable of getting ahead of herself, but she was certain that this was the man she wanted to marry. The only question was, did he feel the same way?

Sitting around the kitchen table the Raber family and their guest joined hands for a moment of silent prayer. On her left, Alison held hands with her mother, but on her right was Nathan. His strong hand easily fit her dainty one in its palm like a set of measuring cups. She tried to focus on her prayer but the feeling of his skin on hers was almost too much. With a sinking feeling in the pit of her stomach she realized Emily felt the same way. She looked down at her lap as in prayer, but the blush across her cheeks and the coy smile gave away the fact that she was just as giddy about holding Nathan's hand as Alison was.

Alison felt a lump in her throat. In a game of wits, she'd beat Emily every time, but one of charm and flirtation was Emily's wheelhouse. The fantasy she had of marrying this man was over. If Emily had the same idea in her head, she would certainly come out on top. Alison felt defeated before she had even begun to try to win Nathan's affections.

At the end of the silent prayer, Nathan squeezed her hand once before letting go. That one small gesture reignited every feeling that she just a moment ago resolved to let go. Did that display of affection mean what she thought it meant? Did he also squeeze Emily's hand? She looked at her sister to see if her face held any indicators, but her back was already to the table as she and Mama began to serve lunch. A million thoughts were racing through her head when Nathan turned to speak to her.

"I'm so glad to have found you yesterday. It's so nice to deliver Maeve's puppies to family's around town and see the joy they bring first hand, especially to a family like yours."

"A family like mine?"

"So welcoming and kind, and intriguing to boot."

"Intriguing, what's so intriguing about us?"

"Well, more you. Your father went on and on about Emily and your mother, but was always less forthcoming about you. When I pressed him on it he got a mischievous twinkle in his eye and just said, 'You'll have to wait and see.' It appears that there are some parts of you that defy explanation and I'm curious to explore them."

The redness bloomed on her face like drops of dye in water. Luckily, Mama and Emily returned to the table with the meal just in time to save her from having to give a response. Did she hear him correctly? It's possible he meant what he said in a friend-like way, many people were curious about her. Some neighbors even treated her like an oddity, testing her with math problems as she walked down the street. But something about the way his lips moved and his eyes pierced straight into hers that assured her of his actual intentions. Their attraction was mutual, but his attraction to her stronger than his attraction to Emily?

"Bread, Nathan? I baked it fresh this morning."

"Thank you, Emily. It smells delicious. I just wanted to thank you all for inviting me into your home. This isn't an easy time for you all; in fact I should be inviting you into my home! You're generosity is something to be admired."

"It's a welcome distraction, dear. We've been awful gloomy around here, understandably, but my husband wouldn't have wanted us to mope about. Our happiness was always his first priority in life and I can't imagine that much has changed in his death."

"That's a mighty fine way to put it, Mrs. Raber."

"You said my husband found you in an ad for puppies. Is that what you do, then? Are you a dog breeder?"

"No, ma'am. Maeve and her beau get a little rambunctious every once in a while and I have to find something to do with the puppies so whenever she has another litter I just throw up a bulletin and pick the most loving families to hand them off to. Maeve and I work on my father's farm in the next town over. She chases the livestock away and I wrangle them back up. We make a great team."

"Will you inherit the farm? In all this sadness I almost forgot that Alison now officially owns the family carriage shop, but that's not that big of a change. She basically ran the thing on her own before anyways."

"You're a business owner?" Nathan asked Alison, unable to mask the surprise in his voice.

"Yes, does that shock you? A woman owning a business?" she didn't mean to be so terse, but this wasn't the first time she had been faced with this sort of reaction. Nathan only laughed.

"No! Of course not. Don't tell my father but I think women should own every business. Things would run so much more efficiently. It's only that every time I learn something new about you I am more and more impressed. You're father wasn't wrong. You are something else."

Alison was a little embarrassed by her outburst, but Nathan seemed to be challenged by it instead of offended. Not one to be outdone, Emily chimed in.

"I don't work at the carriage shop, but some days I'll put together a whole spread of snacks and refreshments for the employees."

"How very thoughtful of you, Emily."

Nathan's reply was kind, but only Alison could pick up on its dismissive tone. Nathan may have squeezed both of their hands, but he was only interested in Alison. She smiled from ear to ear for the first time since her father's passing. She was by no means over his death, but she couldn't help feel like he'd want her to embrace this joy. Papa meant for them to meet. He knew that they'd share this connection.

Uncharacteristically, Alison reached under the table to grab Nathan's hand, out of sight of her mother or Emily. Nathan was surprised but didn't pull away. He turned to her and smiled with his whole face. She squeezed his hand. Angel was a wonderful surprise, but this was something else.

AMELIA OF THE AMISH

MAYA WINSTON

"It really is such a shame how she hasn't found anyone."

"Oh, I know it. And it's not as if she wouldn't make a good wife. She is a lovely young woman."

"True, my dears. But think of where she comes from. No parents to speak of. What man is going to want to tether himself to such uncertainty?"

"Yes, that is a point. Her family history is such a mystery. How can we know that she came from a good family when we don't know where she came from?"

"And that is why I never would have wanted my Julius to court her. He is much better off with his wife. She comes from a good, solid community family."

"It doesn't matter how good of a midwife she is, or how lovely she is. Without that family foundation, she has very little chance of ever being accepted by any of our young men for the long term."

Amelia knew that the old women did not realize that she was close enough to hear them. They sat in this same place before every service speaking in whispered tones. Generally such discussions were not conducted within her earshot, however, on this day she had arrived early and been treated to hearing the hurtful sentiments. These female elders of the community were very influential, and if this was the tone that they were setting in regards to her viability as a wife, then she knew that there would be no hope for her marrying in the community. She tried not to let it bother her. She did her best to not dwell on how unfair it all was, but lately it had been harder to ignore the loneliness at night.

She loved being the community's most sought-after midwife. This station was firmly established now after many years of hard work. She adored working with young women, helping them bring healthy, loved babies into the world. She had been orphaned as a very small child, and the community had wrapped her in their arms and cared for her as their own when an old maid of the community had brought her home when no one else stepped forward to care for her. She had been born to a single mother outside of the community, and Amelia's adoptive mother had thought it the will of the Lord to bring her into their world. And as soon as Amelia realized how different her background was from the children around her, she decided she wanted to be a midwife when she got older. She did not know what being around a family was really like, but she thirsted for even the brief contact that she knew would come as a midwife.

She had worked hard and been a delight to raise and educate for all the adults around them. She was beloved and had many friends in the community. In short, she was one of them, with the glaring flaw of not actually being a member of any "good family" by blood. This did not affect her childhood or friendships much, but when it came time for her to start thinking about suitors, that was when she really understood what her background meant. No amount of hard work would change the fact that she was different, an outsider by blood. She was not Amish by blood. In fact, she was the product of a sinner that had lived the life that their community would never embrace. Allowing sons of the community to court her would be tantamount to allowing them to court women outside of their order, which all knew was not allowed.

So there she sat, listening to the old bitties gossiping about her under the guise of concern, mapping out the course of her future based upon their own notions of what would make a young woman suitable for family life. Her adoptive mother had long since passed, and she didn't have anyone else to speak to about how this all made her feel.

"You are my daughter, Amelia," she had always said. "I don't care what anyone says."

Amelia couldn't help but wonder what life would be like for her if her adoptive mother had lived longer. She had passed before Amelia was old enough to start receiving suitors. She wondered if her adoptive mother were still alive if the community would be more accepting of her. With a chuckle, she answered her own question in her mind. The fierce, loving old maid that had taken in an "English" baby because no one else wanted to would never have stood for the rejection she received from the community. She would have gone to the ends of the earth to make sure that her daughter, because that is what she had become, would find a suitor that not only respected her, but made her happy. But, sadly that was not to be, and she was alone in her struggles.

Amelia had resigned herself to the fact that she would likely follow in her adoptive mother's footsteps and die an old maid. The thought was not all negative, because they had had a fulfilling life together. But, now that she was older, she often wondered if her mother had been as lonely at night as she was every time the sun set over their small corner of the world.

With a deep breath, Amelia made a show walking around the corner, acting surprised to see the women, and feigning complete ignorance about the fact that they had just been speaking about her. The only hint that they had been caught unawares by her presence was a slight bit of extra coloring in their cheeks. They were very good at the whole gossip thing. Her adoptive mother had disliked that part of their community a great deal. If she had something to say, she would do so directly. She said that it saved time on misunderstandings and cleared the air faster than festering resentments.

Amelia just didn't have it in her to be confrontational. She always hesitated to say what was on her mind if she knew that it would hurt someone's feelings or cause drama. Her adoptive mother had always said that it was her greatest gift and her most destructive flaw. She loved unconditionally, and bestowed love upon those that may have not reciprocated. And while that kind of approach to life was what made her a fantastic midwife, it was also quite isolating when she found so little love returned. She had to admit to herself that while she had accepted that she may never marry, it did pain her to know that she would never have that sort of love.

She sat quietly for the service and was as devout as she was always expected to be. She played her part well, and enjoyed the spiritual gifts of her dedication. But she couldn't help but feel as she sat, that there were eyes on her, watching, judging her as a person, as a woman.

When the serviced ended, she smiled for friends, and hugged past patients. She admired the babies that she had helped bring into the world and exclaimed over how big they had all gotten. She had a couple of patients that she needed to check in with, and once that was done, the crowd had started to thin out. Her home was not far from the meeting house, and she said her final good-byes and began to head in the direction of home.

"Amelia, wait please." She turned and saw one of the elder's wives bustling toward her.

"Yes, Sister?"

"Hello, Amelia. I wanted to catch you before you left. We have a new school teacher starting tomorrow morning. He is coming to us from a community in Ohio. He does not have any family here and is arriving this evening. We are asking the women of the community to prepare a dish to bring to his home so that he will feel welcomed and comfortable upon his arrival."

Amelia smiled. In spite of her frustrations with how they saw her worthiness as a spouse, she loved the way the women here took in newcomers and made them feel welcome. Not all Amish communities were so welcoming, and it always made her proud to live in such a special place. "Of course. I would be happy to. What time are the dishes being brought by?"

He is going to be living in the school teacher's home owned by the community, so we told him that we would set it up for him. He should arrive after dark this evening, so any time before then is fine to come and go. The door will be open and the dishes will be trickling in throughout the day."

"That sounds wonderful. I will make sure that I bring something to his new home before nightfall."

The two women parted ways and Amelia headed in the direction of home. She was pleased to have the distraction of a task to bring her away from her thoughts about her own future. Usually her distraction was work, but the few patients that she had waiting to deliver at the moment still had a good long time to go.

She spent that day preparing breads and spreads that she knew would last a few days so that the new school teacher would have time to settle in without having to think of food. As she worked, she reflected upon how strange it felt that there was a young, unmarried male teacher coming into their community. That was an uncommon combination in her Amish world. Generally young men were laborers and farmers that were in search of a wife in their own established community. She wondered what was different about this man. Why would he be searching for a new community at such a point in his life? Why would he want to start over in a new community when he was likely of marrying age? It was a mystery, but not one that she would likely know the answers to until she had the chance to get to know the man. She knew that it was commonplace for people to speculate and gossip about such things, but she found it to be a spectacular waste of time that often led to misconceptions and miscommunication. Still, she was only human, and this was a curiosity because the situation was unusual.

When she was done preparing and carefully packing up the foods that she prepared, she loaded them into a basket and set out to the home next to the school house. The walk was about as long as the one to the meeting house and it was a brisk, refreshing trip. The temperature had dropped and the sun would be setting soon. She let herself into the front door of the small house and looked around. There were baskets and bowls covering much of the kitchen area. It appeared as if she was one of the last women to drop her items off. That was not a surprise though, since they must have know about the teacher's arrival for days and she had just learned of it today.

She placed her basket on the counter and un-wrapped the bread so that it could cool a bit. The home smelled divine with all of the food, but was starting to get dark as the sun outside began to set. She decided that she would light some of the lanterns to make his arrival warmer. She always hated returning to a cold, dark home. There was already a fire warming the hearth, so she figured that her neighbors had the same idea that she did.

As she lit the last lamp, the door opened and in walked the most enticing man that Amelia had ever seen. He was tall and his wide shoulders filled up the doorway. He had to duck slightly to avoid hitting his head on the frame. The lantern light sparkled in his dark eyes, and the hair on his face could not hide high just how handsome his face was.

"Hello," he said in a deep voice. "I hope that I don't have the wrong house. My name is Addison Miller. I'm the new school teacher, and I *did* think that this was going to be my new home." He spoke with a hint of laughter in his voice.

"Hi, Brother Miller. I'm so sorry. I was just delivering a basket of food and thought that it would be nice for you to arrive to some lit lamps, rather than darkness. I always hate coming home to a dark home myself." In her head she thought that she should be embarrassed to be here, alone, with this strange man. But she just couldn't bring herself to feel anything by fascinated. A man such as this being a school teacher was not at all what she had been expecting.

"That is very thoughtful of you. And I hope that you didn't labor over *all* of this food."

"Oh no. Just this basket here." She gestured to her basket.

"Well, I shall enjoy that basket first then, Sister..."

"I'm so sorry. Fisher. Amelia Fisher. I'm the local midwife. I live about a mile and a half down the road leading away from the meeting house." She was flustered. She had completely forgotten her manners. She could not stop staring at this man, trying to riddle him out.

"Well, Sister Fisher..."

"Amelia, please," she interrupted. She didn't know why she was granting a stranger the right to call her by her given name, but it just felt right.

"Well, Amelia, thank you most kindly for your efforts. I do find it nicer to come back to a lit home. Even when there is no one there to welcome me, I still feel as if I am not alone."

Amelia continued to stare, catching and holding his eye. She suspected that she was making him a bit uncomfortable. But she had never heard her own thoughts on the subject so eloquently and succinctly spoken. His words were her words, only she had never spoken hers aloud.

After a long silence, she blinked and cleared her throat. "I completely understand, Brother Miller. I feel very much the same way."

"Please call me Addison, Amelia"

"Addison," she repeated with a small smile. She liked the way his name rolled off her tongue. The sun had now fully set and the shadows cast by the lanterns shaded his face in a mysterious way. Her eyes fell upon his lips and she wondered what it would be like to fall into their warmth and taste. With a jerk of her head, she suddenly came back to herself. "I must go." She could not allow herself to fall any further into such sinful, out-of-character thoughts. She needed to put immediate distance between herself and the temptation that this man had unexpectedly become.

"Let me fetch you a way home. It is cool out tonight and I doubt that you were expecting to be out this far after nightfall."

"Thank you, no. I enjoy a brink evening walk. I have a family to check in on between here and my home, anyway." She smiled again and quickly turned to leave.

"Amelia." His voice stopped her as she reached the doorway leading outside.

"Yes?"

"It was an unexpected pleasure making your acquaintance this evening."

His words caused goose bumps to breakout out up and down her arms. "Likewise, Addison. Welcome to your new home." She passed through the door and headed away from his home without looking back. She was afraid that if she did and saw his silhouette in the soft light from the windows that she would not be able to stop herself from turning around and returning to him and his strong arms. Not only would that would sinful and inappropriate, but quite possibly embarrassing as she didn't think that he would ever feel the same way. If he didn't know about her ineligibility as a wife already, he certainly would soon. She wanted to save herself the pain of rejection by the only man that had ever sparked her fancy. The attraction was visceral, and as such, she knew that she was going to have to stay away from him in order to protect her heart.

* * *

As the next few weeks passed, Amelia threw herself into her work and caring for her home. She had some projects that she had been meaning to get to and this was a good a time as the midwifery season had been a bit slow. Being so busy also had the added benefit of keeping her away from town and Addison Miller. She saw patients, but they usually came to her house, or she went to theirs, so she was still able to avoid town that way. And then when she needed to venture out for supplies, she tried to make quick trips, avoiding conversation and gossip.

It was a fruitless effort, however, because people were talking of nothing but Addison Miller. It seemed that he was generally regarded as the best teacher that their community had even been blessed to welcome. The children of all ages loved him and were already learning things with him that the old school teacher would never have dreamed to introduce. He was progressive in many ways, but not so much that he would anger the more traditional elders of the community. He was giving with his time and helpful to those around him. In short, as far as Amelia was concerned, he was very nearly the perfect man. Or at least he would have been the perfect man for her.

The talk about his considerable attributes was accompanied by speculation about his background and why he was still a single man. He was from a community in Ohio and well regarded as a teacher and a man, or so the story went. It was mentioned how attractive and capable he was, in such a way as to suggest this alone should have meant that he would already be happily married.

"Oh, I think that he would make the perfect match for my sister's daughter."

"The Yoder girl is a good girl to introduce him to, such a good family for a school teacher to be connected to."

"Oh I hope he doesn't decide to move along anytime soon. My Isabella is too young for marriage now, but in a couple of years she will be ready, and he will still be of reasonable age for her."

The discussions were often quite presumptuous, and Amelia wanted to ask if they knew for a fact that he was looking to marry, but she decided to stay mute on the subject. She hated the sympathetic looks that were cast her way whenever the subject of marriage would arise. Those were almost worse than the direct comments about how she shouldn't worry; the community would always be there to support her.

When the days came for worship, she would sneak in at the last moment, and rush out before people had a chance to catch her in a conversation. She imagined that there must be talk about her suddenly anti-social behavior, but she didn't pay that any mind. There was always talk about her anyway.

It had been exactly five weeks to the day when Amelia turned up her front walk to find Addison standing next to her front door when she returned from a post-worship patient visit. She stopped in her tracks and took in the sight of him. She had not been remembering him accurately, she saw now. He was even more handsome and intriguing than she remembered. "Hello, Sister Fisher," he said in a friendly tone.

Amelia was momentarily taken aback that he had referred to her formally, until she saw that there were a couple of people passing by behind her on the street. She appreciated his discretion, considering that familiarity between the two of them would have shocked people since no one else knew of their meeting the month before.

"Brother Miller. How are you this fine afternoon?"

"Well, thank you. I was wondering if I might have a quick word with you."

Amelia took her time answering, making sure that the people walking by were out of sight. "Of course. Come in."

She entered before him and set to putting on a tea kettle after lighting the kitchen lamp. "It's nice to see you, Amelia," he said from a chair at the kitchen table where he had made himself comfortable.

"You too, Addison." She didn't look up when she spoke, but continued to busy herself with the task of making a tea tray.

"Do you really mean that?" His voice was quiet, but his words were terribly loud in her mind. She whipped her head up and took in his face for the first time since they had entered the house. He looked lovely, as usual, but there was a tightness around his eyes that gave away something weighing on his mind.

"Sorry?"

"You say that it's nice to see me, but do you really mean that?"

"I heard what you said. I just don't understand what you mean."

"I just mean that...Well, I have the feeling that you have been avoiding me."

She felt herself pale as his words sunk in. How could be know that she had been avoiding him? Did he also know what an effect their first meeting had had on her? "I don't know why you would think that." She didn't want to lie and say that she hadn't been, but she also didn't want to admit the complete truth.

"I have caught your eye a couple of times in town, but you pretended to not see me and rushed away."

"Oh." Again, she didn't want to lie, but what could she say? It was true.

"And then when I have asked about you in town, people have said that you are usually quite involved and friendly, but have been acting a little strangely lately – keeping to yourself and creating projects that will keep you in your house more often than you used to." His eyes never left her as he spoke. It made her feel like he could see the jumble of confused thoughts in her head.

"I have been busy, that is true." She was cautious with her wording, wondering where this conversation was going.

"Why have you been busy?" His voice was gentle, and made her want to divulge all of the secrets that she had been harboring in regards to not only him, since their first meeting, but also her heartbreak at being considered not good enough to wed by the people that she cared about most in the world.

"I'm just trying to get things ready for the winter around my home since I have a slow season with patients right now." She kept her eyes firmly planted on the table as she spoke; knowing that one look at her eyes would show him that she was not telling him the whole truth.

"Amelia, please tell me the truth. Don't sin by lying to me." His voice was so calm and even, she thought, a bit smug.

She felt her anger rise up at his words. It was one thing for him to ask her the truth, it was quite another for him to question her devoutness or morals. She opened her mouth and couldn't control the words that started to spill out. "You listen here, Addison Miller, and listen well. I have been avoiding you, yes. I felt a connection to you like I have never felt with another man in all of my years. My thoughts about you and about us were the sin that I was trying to avoid by staying away from you. I need to protect my heart. I need to make sure that I can come out the other side of knowing you still intact with my heart and my pride. So, don't you judge me and my motives. You do not have the right to do that, not until you have spent a day or two in my shoes."

If Amelia thought that her outburst would placate or intimidate him in any way, she was very wrong. He stood, red faced and turned away from her as he began pacing between her kitchen and parlor. She let him fume, not wanting to be the first to speak after what she had just revealed.

Suddenly he stopped dead, threw his arms up, and looked at her. "I'm not judging you Amelia. I am, however, not an ignorant man. I felt the same connection that you did. I likely had the same thoughts. I don't understand your reaction though. Why do you think that you would get hurt by getting to know me? Why do you think that your heart and pride would not be intact after all is said and done? Is it because of who I am? Is because I am a school teacher? Is it because I am not the type of man that you want to build a family with? Is it my lack of connections in your community? Am I too progressive?" With each unanswered question, his voice had gotten louder and louder, and he finally just let out a frustrated sigh and rubbed his hands over his face. "This isn't getting us anywhere. Please, Amelia, just tell me what it is." He sounded defeated suddenly, his voice mirroring how she herself felt.

She nodded her head, letting him know that she intended to answer. Then she stood and walked to him. "We cannot explore this any further because there just won't ever be a future for us, and I don't want us to get hurt."

"Why do you keep saying that?" His frustration was rolling off of him in waves. "You just keep saying the same thing without ever giving me a real answer."

"If you were talking to people about me at all, then they must have told you my story. People seem to love to share that with newcomers." She tried to keep the bitterness out of her voice, but was not completely successful.

"You're a midwife that lives alone and is regarded as one of the most talented midwives that they have ever had living in this community."

"Did they tell you anything else about me? Did they tell you about my past? Did they broach the subject of why I'm still single?"

"Whenever the conversation would start to head in that direction I would change the subject or excuse myself. I very much dislike gossip. I find that it leads to misconceptions and half-truths. It can dictate how someone is perceived, even when the information shared is not real or unimportant."

He was again echoing her own thoughts without her ever having spoken them aloud. It was uncanny how much they shared such uncommon thoughts. "I agree with you, but in this case it would have done you well to have listened. Please have a seat." She gestured to the chair that he had previously vacated and sat in her own.

"Alright, but this is worrying me a little bit." He tried to lighten the mood with a chuckle, but failed. She just couldn't bring herself to smile. It would be so wonderful to pretend that the realities about her past didn't matter to this wonderfully attractive man. It would be easier to spend some time with him before he knew, but in the long run that could only lead to more pain.

"I came to this community when I was very young," she started. "I was an abandoned orphan of an English person. I am not Amish by blood. No one really knows anything about the family from which I do get my blood." She held his eyes as he leaned back in his chair. His face gave nothing away, but the fact that the gesture subtly moved his body to a position farther away from hers was not lost on her.

"I was taken in by a kind, caring single woman who was well respected in the community," she continued. She raised me as her daughter and gave me her name, though, as I have been reminded a million times, she could not give me her blood."

He furrowed his brows at that. "What does that mean?"

"I am not eligible to be married in this community," she said plainly.

"For what reason?" He looked genuinely confused, so she continued on.

"I have been told since I was old enough to understand that I will not be marrying any of the men in this community because I have non-Amish blood, and because no one knows if I come from a good family. No one in the community wants to bring children from a mother that may be from a sinful or unworthy family. They often bring it up as it being a 'shame' that I will never marry because I am so talented at midwifery. They use their tongues as weapons to warn off any would-be suitors or young men that show interest. At this point I am labeled. I am a cautionary tale. No one minds me bringing children into the world, as long as they are not mine." This time she didn't even try to mask the bitterness.

Addison was silent as he regarded her. "And how does that make you feel, Amelia?" His voice was quivering with some intense emotion, but she could not read it on his face.

"How would that make you feel, Addison?"

"Why answer a question with a question? I just want to understand your part in this. Are you in agreement with them? Do you think that you are unworthy of building a life simply because you do not share their backgrounds?" She flinched. The emotion that had been boiling in him was anger, and it was no longer suppressed. He was furious.

"Of course I don't believe it. But what can I do?"

"So you play the victim and allow them to tell you how to live your life. You let someone else define how you will be happy? You stay in a community where they will treat you like a second-class citizen?" He was shouting by the end of the rant.

"What choice do I have, Addison? This is home," she shouted back.

He closed his eyes and took a deep breath through his nose. His next words cut her to the core as he growled them through his teeth. "Then you are not the woman that I thought you were, and I seem to have gotten lucky to not have gotten much more involved."

Without another word he turned and walked out of her kitchen and practically launched himself through the door. Amelia was left hurt and stunned. How could he say such a thing? At least she could tell herself that she was right. If she had let herself become close to this man, she would have lost her heart and her dignity. As it stood, she lost only her dignity, her heart was still intact. And she was very angry. Tears burned at her eyes. But they were angry tears, not sad. That was good. Angry tears were tools that could gave her strength when she thought that she was going to give up. He had cut her deeply, but given her renewed strength, which she chose at that moment to see as a gift.

* * *

Two weeks passed quickly after her altercation with Addison in her kitchen. The morning after she had woken with swollen eyes, a sick stomach, and a resolve like nothing she had even experienced. His words had hurt her, but they had also been the truth. She had been letting others determine how she would be happy. She needed to take the reins of her own life and not let the opinions of others shape her choices. She had some decisions to make about where her future would go, but she knew now that it would be her making the decisions – not fear, and not other community members.

She saw nothing of Addison as the first week passed, and only caught a brief glimpse of him at worship. It seemed that it was his turn to avoid her now. She heard that he was settling in well at the school and seemed to be happy in his position.

As the sting of his words began to dull, she realized that the truths that he had spoken were even more troubling. She had spent a great deal of time letting other tell her how she should live her life, and that needed to stop. She began to find her smile again, because whether or not she chose to marry someone in a different community, or she decided to stay and remain unwed, it would be her choice. She knew that she was worthy of whatever she wanted to have, and that was the best realization that she could have ever had. She began to put out inquiries about a possible replacement midwife for the community, just in case.

Three weeks to the day of their last conversation, Addison came knocking on Amelia's door. She was in her kitchen preparing soup to keep her warm as the days were getting colder.

Knock. Knock. Knock.

"Come in," she said, wiping her hands on her apron. When he peeked around the door and pushed his way in, she stopped what she was doing and stared. "What are you doing here?" She had not meant to sound rude, but her surprise had caused her to momentarily forget her manners.

"May I come in, Amelia?" He spoke quietly, as if to placate her.

"Yes. What can I do for you?"

"I was hoping to speak with you for a few minutes. I wanted to clear something up with you."

"Okay. Please sit down. Tea?"

"No, thank you. Please sit with me." She let out a small huff, but relented and took a seat in the same position that she had been in the last time they were here together. "I heard that you are putting out inquiries for replacement midwives. Is that true?" His voice had sadness in it, though she couldn't understand why.

"Yes, I am exploring the idea of moving along to a different community."

"Why? Is it because of what I said?"

"Your words hurt, Addison. I won't lie. But they also solidified something in my mind – I am worthy of making my own choices and becoming a wife if I wish. I don't have to settle just because I like this community. I am going to find happiness for myself too." She had rushed through the speech and looked up only when she finished. What she saw was a complete shock. Addison actually had tears in his eyes.

"I'm sorry that I hurt you. Those words were said in anger and frustration, but I don't believe that you are weak or that you were allowing yourself to be controlled. Not at all. In fact, I believe that you are one of the strongest people I know to stand up in the face of such prejudice and keep going contentedly." He reached for her hand. "Please do not leave because of me and my foolish words."

"Addison, I..."

"Wait, please hear me all the way out and then you can make whatever decision you think is right, just as I knew you always would."

"Alright," she said, and settled back in her chair.

"You and I share not only similar ideas, and an unexplainable connection, but also similar histories. I was the son of an Amish mother and father, however, my father was married to a different woman, and my mother was unwed when she conceived me. My father refused to acknowledge me and he and his family moved away. My mother and I were shunned and she died when I was very young of an illness that she couldn't fight. Her cousin's family took pity on me and raised me, but never as an equal.

"I excelled at schooling and so they sent me away to be a sort of apprentice to a kind school master in the Ohio community where I lived for many years. I was respected as a good teacher and kind man, but never seen as the sort of person a nice Amish girl from a good

Amish family should wed. So I lived in the shadow of that warning for many years, until one day I decided that I should leave and pursue a life in a place where my identity as a 'bastard' was not known. I thought that I might start fresh.

"And then I met you. I knew that we were meant to meet the minute I saw you standing in my kitchen that first night. I knew that you belonged there. I suddenly knew why God had brought me to this place in particular. And that was why I was so angry when you told me of your acceptance of your fate. I saw myself in that acceptance and it made me afraid. I should have told you then and there, but I was a fool and lashed out at you, as if I was looking at myself in a mirror."

Amelia stared at him in utter disbelief. Tears rolled down her face, and rather than being appalled at what he had shared, she saw hope like never before.

"Are you saying, then that you would disregard the opinions of the elders and marry someone like me?"

He reached out her hand and held her gaze with his own. "In a heartbeat, my darling. If you'd have me. I am just like you."

She considered him for a long moment and thought about all that she knew of her own history and his. "Addison, I am not sure how to say this to you."

He looked down at the ground. "Okay."

"Please look at me," she said, reaching for his face and guiding his gaze back to hers. "I think that after what you have told me there is no doubt left. There are no two people in the world better suited for one another, and I think we have waited long enough to start making our futures."

The shock that flashed in his eyes pleased her, and the kiss that followed as he swept her into an embrace melted away any doubt that she had left. She was home, and she had found a man that would live there with her. She no longer had to settle, and neither did he. They had both been blessed with nothing short of a perfect match.

www.ingramcontent.com/pod-product-compliance
Lightning Source LLC
Chambersburg PA
CBHW021442150726
47989CB00001B/347